They Won't Apologize for the Mess

ISBN 979-8-9913308-0-0 (Paperback)
ISBN 979-8-9913308-1-7 (Hardback)
ISBN 979-8-9913308-2-4 (eBook)
Library of Congress Control Number: 2024918188
First Edition
The story and all names, characters, and incidents portrayed in this production are fictitious. No identification with actual persons (living or deceased), places, buildings, or products is intended or should be inferred—with the exception of the tornadoes and the sinkhole. Those are real. Be careful out there.

Visit the author's website at www.XineRose.com

Published by BirkenStacks: www.BirkenStacks.com

An imprint of Castle of Air: www.CastleofAir.com

For those eating their cake.

"From woman came corruption."
-Emperor Theophilus

"And from woman came the most excellent."
-Saint Kassiani

CONTENTS

PROLOGUE

March, 2012

A gospel radio station in Eastern Kentucky is interrupted each Monday night by a man who smokes a pack a day, drives an Astro Van and has superstitions about white lighters. He never can decide what his DJ name should be. So he goes by his Christian name, the name his mother gave him: Hunter.

Now this is a gospel radio station, mind you. If Hunter is going play songs no one wants to hear, then he must play them when everyone has gone to bed which means Hunter is tasked with lulling his home town to sleep with the best of the profane.

If Jesus said love your neighbor, then Hunter says, love your neighbor's music. So Hunter leaves no genre left behind. He finds notable connections between songs using guitarists, guitars, political history, artwork, cowbells, studio locations, films, dogs, myths, rumors and women. Especially women. "Everything leads back to a woman," he says, at least three times a night.

A college radio station in San Francisco invites him to guest-DJ for three days. His friend Frankie moved to San Francisco with a woman several years prior. California stuck but the woman didn't, so Hunter has a place to stay. Despite his mother's protests, Hunter drives for four days in his 1993 Astro Van, sleeping at rest stops on a mattress in the back. A cashier at a Flying J tells him he's driving the 37th parallel across the country. Tells him to be careful: it's some sort of paranormal highway.

Hunter is a bit disappointed when nothing happens, not even a late season snow storm. When he misses a turn and manages to drive into the city from the north, San Francisco greets him with stopped traffic on the Golden Gate bridge.

The traffic crawls forward to reveal two people pulled off on the side of the road. There is no fender bender, or emergency vehicles. Just two people embracing each other as their car sits, blocking two lanes, doors wide open. *Ding Ding Ding.*

"Hide and Seek" plays over Hunter's radio. He has witnessed a movie scene in real life, no dialogue, just a vision with a soundtrack. It's not paranormal by any means, but it is something.

As he continues his drive, he tries to prepare for his guest spot. He really does. He makes audio notes of lyrics and guitar riffs on his phone. He plays a couple of songs over his car radio. But he loses focus every time a man sings about a woman. He wonders, are songs about women, written by men, the metaphorical rib plucked from their chest? Is it the man's curse to take the best thing from them, and pluck it out? Over and over, for eternity?

He doesn't prepare a playlist for his show. He decides to wing it. For him, working on the fly is a religious experience, a leap of faith and a public act of worship. Or maybe it is a taste of the forbidden fruit.

When he settles into the studio, his routine begins like a liturgy; adjusting first the headphones, then his seat and microphone. A tattoo on his hand says *damn right, they'll rise again.* Is it a blatant prophecy? Or is it more like a wish made as a coin is tossed into a fountain, or a whispered prayer as his pointer finger hovers over the ON AIR button.

Regardless, the beginning of a story sneaks into the room with him. It's as if the theatre lights dim right in the middle of his young adult life. The curtains are drawn as he presses the button that sends his voice through the radio towers to the greater San Francisco area. A once-upon-a-time is stirred by the nervous bounce of his knee. An infant wind grows as the first song reverberates. West coast air becomes unstable, riding the coattails of a cold front. This eastward wind develops into a herd of tornadoes in the Ohio Valley region, where I am—where my soul is at stake.

Monday Night Playlist

TRACK 1: "SHE DON'T USE JELLY"

New Year's Eve, 2012

There is a receiving line through my apartment, like after a wedding ceremony, but instead of a newly married couple, it is only me and my unhappy ending. Which is funny because my name is Story.

"Free at last!" My roommate's sister winks at me.

"Sweet freedom!" My roommate's date tonight fist pumps the air.

The good intentioned cheers echo through our apartment which, thanks to my roommate, Jodie, has been converted into a chapel honoring the desecration of marriage—a ceremony of untying the knot. Everything unholy is lifted with praise and blessed with wine. The party hats celebrate how much fun it is to have forsaken my vows. The penis-shaped wine-glass charms symbolize both the shameful lack of vagina-shaped wine-glass charms and all the fornication I will commit guilt-free now that I am no longer "tied down." Then, there is my wedding cake sitting on the Formica countertop, waiting for its fate. The plan is to light it on fire or blow it up: whatever a group of drunk adults can manage to do in the parking lot before the cops are called. It hasn't done anything to deserve this: I am the hell-bound sinner.

I approach the freezer-burnt clump of buttercream icing, like it might shudder a breath of protest. The cake topper is M.I.A. but I remember what it looked like: two stock figures, one female, one male; one in white, one in black; not unlike Adam and Eve, formed from a mold that has been cast and cast and cast until the seam is visible and off by 2 millimeters. The two figures are skewed, their front sides not quite meeting up with their backsides. A flaw that is imperceptible to anyone who hasn't photographed a hundred couples and their cake toppers like I have.

Where the topper was ripped off, the icing is missing. The cavity reveals a dry and crumbly cake interior. How has it not collapsed already? This thing will burn very quickly or not at all and I fear both outcomes.

There is *something* about the cake though, like a ghost of hope. It bubbles up in my gut like champagne, and with it, comes heat in my cheeks and thoughts of Hunter.

Hunter.

I laugh to myself as I recall two nights prior, only the second time we'd met. I was so surprised and nervous, I lied to him and said I was having a New Year's Eve party. *That he should come.*

How ridiculous, to think he would either come to my New Year's Eve party, or that he wouldn't realize it was a divorce party the moment he walked in. I am still laughing at myself when a hand touches my shoulder.

"Story, are you okay?" Jodie asks, and only then do I realize my nose is inches from the cake on the counter.

I straighten my spine and lie. "Splendid."

"You're thinking about Hunter, aren't you?" Jodie's lips curve, all knowing. "Do you think he'll show up?"

My smile dissolves, and I shake my head no.

"Why not?" Jodie pouts.

"Because only couples celebrate New Year's Eve. Only couples kiss at midnight." I count my fingers. "I had a one-night stand with him ten months ago. He's not going to spend New Year's Eve with me."

"You are *sooo* superstitious," she laughs. "You act like a kiss at midnight is some commitment to intertwined fates."

"Or a curse," I say, barely audible.

"Story." Jodie clutches my shoulder and leans in. "I invited Paul. The beautiful but dumb vending machine stock-boy at my hotel. I am going to kiss him at midnight and then let him fuck me with my underwear still on, like high schoolers behind the bleachers. Will it be worth having to find a new vending stock-boy?" Jodie shrugs, her shoulders framing her coy smile.

I can imagine the sequence of events with ease. Paul, the sweetest, farm-raised gentleman, believing all night he is the luckiest man to be with the exotic woman that runs the nicest hotel in a small town. The woman with all the best beds. Jodie will tell him to pull on her rainbow tipped afro like bridle reins. She will say things like, *harder*, *faster*, and he will come too quickly because she is a lot to please—a quick burn.

I know this because the walls of our apartment are very thin.

"Maybe I don't want another one-night stand," I say.

"Ahhh," Jodie clenches her fists as if she has finally unlocked my secret desires, "So, you *want* him to kiss you at midnight with meaning."

"Slow down," I say. "He is not going to come. Even if he were to, you've forgotten a little detail. This is my *divorce* party. Wouldn't it be a bit of a turnoff if he shows up and finds out that I cheated on my husband with him, and I am celebrating that fact by blowing up my wedding cake?"

Jodie thinks very hard. "We'll just say it's my divorce party."

I would entertain the idea, but her hat says *Ding, Dong, the Dick is Gone*. A laugh escapes me as a snort, and I confess, "He will think we hate men."

"Fine," she says. "We will rip it all down and pretend that we like men. And marriage. We will be God-fearin' women that make our daddies proud."

We laugh because our fathers are alcoholics, ruined by patriarchy in the media and confused by the matriarchy of our rural heritage. The mothers form and shape this region. It is my mother who stays with my helpless father. It is she who ultimately helped me end my marriage—handed me the proverbial fruit.

I wonder what Hunter's mother is like. She must be kind because Hunter is kind. Goodness like that must be passed on like recessive genes, like rewards for past lives. Such rewards are out of my reach. I am glad he's not coming. I want my sacrilegious party. I want to have my cake and blow it up too. I have worked too hard to be distracted by some shiny man-toy with soft hands and kind eyes and a soul that radiates a heat that melts the glaciers from the grooves in my clavicles.

"Hey." Paul approaches, gesturing with his hand. "Want me to get it?"

"What?" Jodie asks. Suddenly the music and the hum of conversation is loud and it is hard to hear Paul.

"The door. Someone is at the door." Paul shakes his finger toward the entrance to our apartment. "Want me to get it for you?"

The shadow of a figure stands outside the frosted glass of our front door.

Jodie's eyes widen as they look at me. I am not surprised when she dips into her country accent. "Well, hell-fire!"

My wide eyes on Jodie tell her I don't believe what is happening.

Jodie is practically dancing on her toes.

"We have to—" I manage to say, but I am all nerves, the good and the bad—the raw and the numb.

"I know." Jodie claps her hands as she walks backwards away from me.

"Jodie—" but my thoughts race and when they aren't forced through my vocal cords they choke me.

"I know, destroy all evidence," she says as she shoots double finger-guns at me.

Jodie whispers instructions to our guests. I witness banners ripped from the walls. The wedding cake is wrapped in aluminum foil and crammed into the freezer. Jodie runs hot water over penis shaped ice cubes. There is a moment in the mad rush that Jodie laughs and waves me over to watch with her as the testicles shrivel in the sink.

Our doorbell rings again. Our apartment goes silent. Everyone looks at me. My pulse is in my ears and it is slow, like I am fading. My heart is not keeping up. I am light headed, and I feel a turbulence in my stomach going the wrong way up my esophagus. I barely make it to the bathroom and lift the toilet seat. When I throw up, it is fast and effortless like an exorcism. Carlo Rossi sangria wine mixes with a handful of crackers. It looks back at me like a tea-leaf reading. Burgundy shapes morph, float, and sink into the toilet bowl. I have a vision of falling into darkness, beneath the surface of the earth. I know with out knowing, Hell is coming for me. I am tangled up with blue....Wait. Blue? What *in Hell* is blue?

The vision disappears, leaving only the pungent remains of my stomach.

When there is a knock on the bathroom door, it is Jodie. I sense Hunter is somewhere on the other side of the door, in our apartment, looking at our secondhand couch, our cardboard coffee table, our stained carpet, peeking into my bedroom at my unmade bed. I flush the toilet as Jodie slips into the bathroom with me.

She is quiet as I stare forward at a tray of nick-nacks on the back of the toilet. I pick up a seashell. When I rub my thumb across it, I still find sand. When I hold it to my ears, I hear the sound that I have always confused for the ocean. Now I know it is the sound of the wind at the top of a fifty-foot cliff, carrying the echo of traffic crossing a bridge in the distance. I close my eyes and remember Hunter faintly lit by a cell phone, his previously combed over hair falling into his face, like an off duty altar boy, naked, smelling of sex—sex with me—and he is playing me love songs through his car radio.

"You know what I think your problem is?"

Jodie's question brings me back to our dingy bathroom, and I return the shell to its tray.

"I think you're afraid of something good happening to you. You're afraid he wants to kiss you at midnight and he wants it to mean something too."

"Well, if he kisses me now, I'm afraid I'm going to taste like vomit." I push myself up to my feet and turn to the sink. I do not recognize myself in the mirror. My hair, once bright tangerine, is now faded like a reheated fish stick. My skin glistens in post-vomit sweat and my lips are chapped.

Jodie hands me a jar of Vaseline. I apply it to my lips and the glossy sheen only adds to my feverish look, like death is around the corner, like my soul is at stake. I can't shake the feeling that bad things are gonna happen. My doctor's advice is to focus on my breathing, eat better, drink more water, and stretch a little. I don't know how a healthy diet can make me a good person. Obviously, my doctor can't save my soul.

"Is he inside?" I ask Jodie.

Her smile tells me yes.

"How much of the divorce party did he see?"

"None," she says, her smile widening as she looks at me.

"You're enjoying this aren't you?"

"You're stalling," Jodie says.

I am stalling. I am not quite ready to leave the bathroom and face the only mistake I don't regret this year.

"He cleans up nice," Jodie says. "When we saw him on stage, I thought, yeah he looks like he lives in a van. But now? Now I'm not so sure he couldn't run for mayor. That boy has come dressed to impress."

I ask her, "What does that mean?"

She nods to the door. I crack it open and scan the apartment. When I find Hunter, my breath catches. He is in a suit and tie with his hair combed over. He holds a bottle of wine in one hand and a bouquet of roses in the other. He looks like he has been cast from a goddamn wedding cake topper.

TRACK 2: "PORTIONS FOR FOXES"

There is cornstarch everywhere. Plastic wine glasses roll slowly across the dirty linoleum floor, sprinkling drops of red wine. It is either a Christmas wonderland or a wintery murder scene.

I am surprised that Hunter hasn't left yet. I refused to kiss him at midnight. *Who comes to a party on New Year's Eve and walks away without a kiss?* Maybe he thinks he can change my mind. He has waited with me, until everyone else has either left or passed out. We are the last ones standing.

He has shed his coat and tie. His slicked-back golden hair is powdered white and starting to curl at the ends. The cornstarch makes him cough, but he smiles through it. He looks like he has been cut and pasted from a classic black and white movie. Film artifacts speckle in the fluorescent lights, before me he is soft and glowing. An analog beauty in a digital world. If he would stay in one place, all the furniture would shutter and spin around on its toes just to face him.

And for some reason, I am behaving like a dragon guarding secrets. My mouth is filled with cornstarch. I lift a lighter in front of my lips, strike the flint and blow the powder through the flame towards the ceiling.

Whoosh!

A flame burns through the cornstarch quickly and brightly, barely licking the textured ceiling before going out.

"You're getting good at that, Fish Sticks." Hunter watches the remaining cornstarch descend like snowfall. I wash out the pasty remains from my mouth with sangria so that I can properly taste the nickname he's given me, "Fish Sticks. Fish Sticks."

"Sorry." He laughs. "Do you prefer I call you Story?"

"No. Fish Sticks is fine." I smile, remembering the taste of grease licked from fingertips.

"Fish Sticks: the fire-breathing dragon," he says, squinting with slouched shoulders, exuding sex.

"That suits me," I say matter-of-factly. "I am a frozen meal with strict instructions that still never turn out quite like you hope. And, I have a reputation for terrorizing townsmen." I should leave it there, but I have lost my inhibition. "I'm dangerous for your health. Dangerous for your soul. Beware! Wear your seat belt. Check your oil." I'm not even sure I'm saying anything aloud anymore.

"Are you drunk or tired?" He laughs, head tilted at me.

There is cornstarch in his wine. It is obvious he hasn't touched it in a while, which means he is not as drunk as I am. His button up is buttoned up. I wonder if my fire breathing skills can burn up the threads of the buttons and open up his shirt in a fiery instant.

"Probably, yes. A little of both." I confess.

He pulls two cigarettes from their pack on the counter. He motions to me as if to ask, *Want one?*

I nod, savoring the experience of communicating with him without words.

He lights them both and holds one out towards me, his hand not quite extended far enough. He is trying to draw me in with his cigarette, and his shoulders, and his side smile—like he doesn't know I am bad news.

"Was that your plan?" I ask, taking his bait. "To keep me up all night?" I collect the cigarette without my hands. My lips barely brush the pads of his fingers.

"We can go to bed whenever you want," Hunter's fingers slip into the pocket of my denim shorts and pull me closer. His scent—tobacco and leather—fills my nostrils, taking me back to California when he thought I was someone I wasn't.

I let him untuck my plaid shirt and unbutton it. My shirt slips over my shoulders as I watch him watch me, cornstarch on his eyelashes like a morning dew, a new day. He puts out his cigarette in an ashtray behind him. My skin is dusted with cornstarch and I look like a ghost. He traces the contours of my skeleton. His fingers draw a map of his gaze, where he slows for inspection or admiration. His inked hand stops at my only tattoo.

"Is this new?" He asks. Ten months is a long time to remember someone's body.

I hesitate at first, letting the seconds draw out as long as I can, filling my lungs with his cologne and the sweet aroma of sangria. "More like bad news," I say in my exhale.

"Bad news?"

We both stand still. He searches my gaze. I avert my eyes. My body feels the force of two north poles repelling: vulnerability and pain.

"There's something in the freezer I need to show you."

"The freezer?" Hunter grimaces.

I laugh because he looks like I am about to show him food that has gone bad. Or maybe he thinks I am about to show him cut up body parts. I remind myself that he doesn't know me that well. I have no idea what he thinks I might be hiding.

"Actually…" I pull away from his grasp. "Maybe I should start at the beginning."

Hunter reaches for me, as if to pull me back in.

I push away, insisting, "This is important."

"How far away is the beginning?"

"March, maybe?" I say, feigning uncertainty.

"When we met?"

"Just before," I say.

"How long does your hot water last?" he asks, leaning back against the kitchen counter.

My mouth opens and then closes. My mind doesn't compute the jump from everything I want to tell him—my sins, my curse, my unworthiness—to the capacity of our water heater.

"What if we talk and shower?" he asks while his footsteps in the cornstarch on the floor lead away from me.

I blink.

"Sort of a two-birds-one-stone situation," he says, already unbuttoning his shirt. His chest hair appears and I am fighting an urge to approach him and run my fingers through it. As he steps away from me, I follow.

"What if what I say changes your mind about me?" I ask him.

"I don't think that will happen," he says.

His certainty feels like a challenge. I am charged by the words, given permission to test his theory. I unbutton my denim shorts. Pull them down over my hips. When they fall to my ankles, I kick them off. I ask him, "Did you ever wonder what I was doing when we met?"

He is unbuttoning his own pants, shaking his head no.

"Have any theories?" I ask, peeling fishnet stockings away.

"You looked very professional in your white collared shirt. Like a traveling Mormon." His pants fall to the tops of his untied boots. He tries to kick them off but trips over the threshold and falls into the bathroom floor. "Oh no, you're a Mormon, aren't you?"

I laugh despite myself and throw my fishnets at him still sprawled on the floor of the bathroom, still fighting his second boot. "Do you even know what I do?"

Once he gets the boot and his pants removed, he returns to his feet, ego barely tarnished. "You were, um, photographing a wedding, I think." He reaches into the shower and turns it on.

In undies and a mis-matched bra, I lean against the door jamb of the bathroom and cross my arms. "Yeah, but that wasn't the only reason. I had another reason."

He approaches me half-smiling, in only boxer briefs. He reaches around me and unclasps my bra. His warm breath is on my shoulder. He carefully removes my bra, folding it and placing it on the vanity sink with reverence, like he is preparing me for a baptism. Then his fingers slip into the waistband of my underwear and I know we are both hell-bound sinners. Neither of us are making it out of the bathroom with our souls intact.

"And then there was no mystery left." I say, in a sing-song voice, my toes clutching the threads of the bathmat as if I could hold the moment there—just before I accept what I must do.

He nudges me into the shower.

For a brief moment, I am chilled flesh and goosebumps. As the hot water hits me, it washes away my powdered armor. I close my eyes and focus on the heat. When I open them again, Hunter is in the shower with me, standing a breath away. Our bodies are streaked with cornstarch and tinted in tungsten from the bathroom light.

"You said you were going to start at the beginning," he says, his eyes darting back and forth between mine.

"Right." I pray that the hot water will last, even though I don't think anyone is listening. "Once upon a time there was a tornado," I say, water streaming down my face.

"I think it's important that you know, I've already seen Wizard of

Oz. I know how it ends." Hunter's teeth flash in the steam.

This is something I'm picking up on, about Hunter. How he is so eager to interrupt, just to get a smile out of me. It's what makes this so hard.

I remember making the same joke before I got on the plane, before I made the biggest mess of my life, and then tried to leave it all behind in Kentucky. I think it's important, that Hunter know what kind of person I was—still am.

TRACK 3: "FIFTY WAYS TO LEAVE YOUR LOVER"

March, 2012

One morning, I woke up to a Post-it note that said, *Sober up. Storms are coming.*

It was stuck to one of the many beer cans on my nightstand. I ripped it off, crumpled it into a ball, and threw it across the bedroom. My phone buzzed with a text from my mom, but I ignored it. I checked my work email as if being wanted by a bride or groom for wedding photography was my best chance to feel desirable.

As if I had asked the universe for a sign and it answered, I had an email marked *URGENT*. It was a referral from a friend in California. Her clients had rescheduled their wedding date due to a family emergency. She wasn't available for their new wedding date, or didn't want to take the pay cut. It was a last minute DIY wedding, which meant it was likely not a big showy affair. That meant it wouldn't boost anybody's portfolio.

My friend knew what she was doing, though. She knew I could still make money even after traveling across the country. That was the price difference between a Kentucky wedding and a California DIY wedding. It was tempting. I replied to the email and said I would have to get back with her in an hour, which was an arbitrary amount of time. All I was going to do in an hour was think about being the kind of person who said *Yes! I'd love to!* for just long enough to not feel bad about inevitably depriving myself of something more fun than drinking all weekend.

My fingers robotically navigated to the little red notification on my messages, and I read my mom's message.

Pick up your father when you wake up. I'll pay you back for bail.

It had been a year since I had been asked to pick up my father. He had been doing so well. Something about it felt unavoidable, though. As if my father's failure could seep through my genes like a leaky oil pan.

There was no use texting Mom back. She would be in a foul mood. The only person she could talk to with any kindness was a patron saint. I threw my blankets off and dressed in boots and a coat like I was off to put out a house fire. The tires on my 1995 C-Class squealed pitifully as I pulled out of the apartment parking lot.

Jail wasn't far from my house. That's why Mom always called me. I lived in a wet county, and they didn't. So, Dad always found his way to my county. After an ambitious tab at the liquor store, he'd get pulled over the moment his truck tires hit the bypass.

The receptionist greeted me before I even crossed the threshold of the jail, "He's already left."

"What do you mean he's left?"

"He's not here, honey."

"He has his truck?"

She stood up from her desk, "No, honey. That got impounded."

I stared at the woman. Her name was Grace and my dad bought roof trusses from her father's business. He also worked on their trucks. Her hair had whitened over the years, but for the most part, she had kept a young face. It gained ten years when she looked at me.

"He paid bail and started walkin'."

I stomped to the car and slammed my door like a child. I was a child. Every daughter is a child chasing after their father.

Inside a cinderblock building with only one small window, across another threshold, I found my dad laughing at the bar inside the liquor store. The store owner saw me coming.

"Looks like your ride's here."

My dad's squinting face spun around on a bar stool to assess me.

"Story!" He flung an arm in the air as if to hug an old friend—a drinking buddy. His other arm stayed on the countertop, his fingers clutching a well whiskey, neat.

"Come on, Dad," I said, not moving into his hug.

His face faltered subtly.

Guiltily perceptive, I approached him with an arm extended out for a side hug and added, "I gotta get you home before it's the dog house for you."

The bartender laughed with him, and I felt a ping of jovial brotherhood that made me feel like I blended in.

"I think it's too late for that. Otherwise, your mom wouldn't have left me to rot in that jail." He said *your mom* as if it was somehow my fault by coming from her vagina.

"It's only been one night, Dad." I laughed. "If you wanted to avoid jail, you probably should have—"

"Sweet talked the sheriff?" My dad interrupted. "Couldn't. Got pulled over by some new cop."

"They've damn near replaced the whole police force," the bartender chimed in, an elbow on the counter with a toothpick bouncing around on his bottom lip.

"Damn shame. Nothin' but kids runnin' the place now." My dad shook his head and finished off his glass. "Another one, please."

I gave my best *don't-you-dare* look at the bartender, which was nothing compared to my mother's and, while still side hugging my dad, tried to pull him off the bar stool and towards the door.

"Let's get you home to your bed, how about that?" I said.

"Nah," he said, even though he was just drunk enough I could probably push him over.

"Yeah, let's go."

"Nah, I'm better off here."

"Don't you want a good night's rest?" I asked, not relenting with my tug towards the exit.

"Sure as hell do," he said, laughing to himself, "and I ain't gonna find that at home."

He wrestled out of my grip and grabbed the counter with both hands. "Another one, bartender."

The bartender didn't move and didn't look at my dad.

"See, Dad, even he thinks you should leave," I said, gesturing to the man.

"Nah, I didn't say that," the bartender said to my dad.

I rolled my eyes. I had almost forgotten. Two old white men will never side with the next generation. To them, we're still tryin' to fix what ain't broke.

"Damn, I will need some cigarettes." My dad patted his shirt pockets and looked to the bartender. "How much are your Marlboros?"

"Five and some change," he said around the toothpick.

"Five dollars?" My dad clutched his chest. "Hell. You know I can just walk down to the gas station and get them for three."

The bartender shrugged. "Won't hurt my feelings."

"Story." My dad swung around to look at me.

I stood with my arms crossed. "Dad."

"What's the weather lookin' like?"

"The weather is gettin' bad."

"Oh yeah?" My dad was drumming his fingers on the countertop. "Is that what the weatherman is sayin'?"

"That's what he's sayin'."

He looked back to the bartender.

"Come on, Dad," I said. "I'd sure like to know you were home safe before the storms come."

He ignored me, threw a crinkly bill on the counter, and whispered to the bartender.

"Dad," I said to his crooked spine.

The bartender grabbed the bill, threw a cigarette pack down, and grab a bottle of whiskey.

There was a tremble to my hands when I tried to uncross my arms, so I kept them crossed. I wasn't waiting impatiently, so much as I was holding myself together.

"Come on, Dad, let's go wash the Corvette, check the fluids, and make sure she doesn't need anything."

My dad watched the bartender pour whiskey and slide the glass back to him.

"One of these days, I'll talk you into puttin' the wheels back on her. Gettin' her off those blocks." I said this because this is what I always said. This was our thing. Talking and dreaming about driving the Corvette again. It was code for *everything will be okay.*

This time my dad didn't let go of the glass. He sat back on the stool with his back to me.

"Come on, Dad—"

"Go home, Story," he said over his shoulder. "If the weather's getting bad, you better get on. I'll not have you worryin' about me."

I wanted to speak but I couldn't believe he wasn't playing his part. He wasn't responding with banter about the Corvette. He wasn't hugging me with a drunken proud smile. He wasn't moving from the bar top.

"Bullshit, old man," I said, bolder. "You're not worried about me. You're only worried about yourself."

The movement in his shoulders did not show an apology or defense. They only told me he was taking another sip of whiskey. I had lost.

I didn't storm out in anger so much as in fear of crying. When I got in my car, I even waited, like he might storm out after me. He might feel bad. He might sense my pain.

When I realized he wasn't coming out, I put the car in reverse and rolled away slowly, thinking about how the universe always waits until the last minute to tell you you were right all along.

The radio DJ was talking about the weather. I shut it off and, then, brought it back on. Meteorologists from the Ohio Valley were watching a "high shear" system. Warm fronts and low-pressure fronts. Tornado warnings for Kansas and Tennessee. Monitoring a storm later in the week.

I shut off the radio again, just in time to hear my phone buzzing in the passenger seat.

"Story?" My mom's voice was frantic.

"Hey, Mom."

"Did you just forget about your dad today?"

A laugh burst through my nose. "No. I tried."

"What do you mean you tried?"

"I tried to get him," I said. "He wouldn't come."

"You're telling me he'd rather stay in jail?"

"No." My hand instinctively went to my forehead where I picked at the skin—practically hunting for pus filled pores. "No, he was at the liquor store when I found him."

She was silent, but I could see her as clear as day, looking out her kitchen window. Looking at her yard that needed weed-eated, needed the gravel re-done, and needed the oil stains cleaned up. Looking at that damn Corvette on blocks that needed to be gone for good.

"I'll get him," she said and hung up.

***

Hunter lights a cigarette in the shower.

"So, then," I say, "I decided I didn't want to be at home—or in Kentucky. I sent an email saying I would take on the wedding if they gave me travel and three days' accommodation."

Hunter is nodding in understanding but is struggling to open the small window in the shower, that I didn't even know opened.

"You're really going to let in the cold air?"

Hunter blows his smoke out the window. "Of course, a window in a shower is the best thing in the world. It's like a hot tub in the winter."

I shiver as my nerves become hyper aware of the heat and chill swirling between us. My warm, pruney hand reaches for winter air.

"I have a lot of questions, and I can't decide," Hunter says between puffs of smoke.

I playfully look around for a pen. "Let's write them all down and draw them out of a hat."

A quick laugh bursts from Hunter, but he sobers quickly. "Do you have a drinking problem?" Hunter's head is slightly bowed so his gaze doesn't strike me like a cannonball, more like a sack of flour with a tear in it. The force dissipates easily enough and I can answer him honestly.

"I may have, then. Yes."

Hunter nods. "Did you get help?"

"What? Like, AA meetings?"

Hunter nods.

"I think we are getting off track. What I'm trying to say is, I was miserable, and perhaps I wished something would happen to give me the push I needed to leave home and not come back. I was past wishing for something good. I was in the market for tornadoes and snowstorms. Hell, I was seeking out the devil himself."

"Or herself," Hunter says, like it is a statement of gender equality.

"No," I say. "Himself."

TRACK 4: "I BELIEVE I'LL DUST MY BROOM"

It was like my mom could sense my retreat. She called me before I put the car in park at the airport.

"Now, tell me again what you're doin'?"

"I have a wedding tomorrow."

"Tomorrow?"

"Yes, in California."

"California?"

"Yes."

"Well," my mom said in her typical *ain't-that-something* tone through the speaker of my cell phone. "And you know that they are calling for tornadoes all over Kentucky?"

"I know," I said as I looked out from my parking spot on the top level of the Cincinnati airport parking garage.

"I guess the weatherman is awfully busy this week. It looks like tornadoes in every direction out there. I'm wondering if I'm gonna have to board up the windows myself."

"I'm surprised Dad hasn't already," I said, checking how greasy my bangs were in the rearview mirror.

"He's still indisposed," she said in a whisper, like someone would hear her.

The airport loomed in the distance through the dusty windshield of my car; a plane just beyond it sped down the runway. My hand mirrored it, fingers flat as its nose tilted skyward, sharper and sharper and then swinging wide to the south and disappearing into large gray clouds.

"Can't you get someone else to photograph it? Someone already in California?"

My hand fell limp. "I'm already at the airport, Mom, and that's not really how the wedding industry works."

"Alright." My mom punctuated the statement with a loud sigh. "It'd be nice to only have to worry about one thing at a time. Now I have to worry about you flying tonight."

"Ah, don't worry about me. And don't worry about the tornado. It worked out for Dorothy, didn't it?"

"Excuse me?" Her tone was like a lightning bolt in soft rain. "Is this a joke to you?"

I leaned forward to rest my head on the steering wheel. "My bad. I just have a very healthy suspicion of weathermen. That's all," which was saying too much.

"Everything alright?"

"Yeah, fine," I said. "I'm just tired."

"You know what they say. When you get to the end of your rope ..." my mom started. My eyes immediately darted to the ragged and filthy stretch of knotted rope on my key ring—the knotted rope keychain from a vacation Bible school. I had made one for Mom and Dad, proudly giving everyone the advice the youth leader had given me: *When you get to the end of your rope, tie a knot in it and hang on!*

Like the thought had just hit her, my mom blurted out, "You're coming back, though? Right?"

It shocked me when she said it. Like I'd been caught pacing outside a bank, with a mask and a fake pistol in my hand. I hadn't done anything yet, but I also didn't know where the mask and pistol came from.

A panicked laugh burst out of me. "Of course."

"Sorry. This weather has my nerves all messed up. I can't think straight."

"Weathermen are wrong all the time," I told my mom. "At the end of the day, there's only so much mere humans can do in the face of nature. Get your rosary out. Pray to the pope or whatever you Catholics do. Everything will be okay," I said, with no conviction.

"Well, kiddo." She sighed loudly, as if to blow the guilt through the cell towers at me. Then, to my surprise, she added, "You're right."

"I gotta go, Mom. I'm at the airport."

"Let me know when you land?"

"I don't think there will be cell service in Oz, mom."

"Very funny." I could hear her eye roll in the jingle of her earrings, and then, like a plea, she said, "I love you, sweetie. I'll see you when you get back."

I hung up with shaking hands as I watched a plane disappear into an expanse of silvery, gray clouds like a swirling crystal ball.

Rolling carry-ons buzzed around me like swarms of plastic bees inside the airport. All flights were held on the ground because debris was spotted in the air. TV screens recycled images of the Ohio Valley covered in green and red technicolor swirls. The urge to turn and go back home zigzagged above my head like a butterfly—erratic and fleeting.

I went to the bar to kill time, choosing a seat next to an older man.

He said, "Hello, darlin'," in this seductive, cigar-smoking, weathered-blues-musician kind of way.

"Hi," I said curtly, keeping my eyes on my fingers as I hunted my pockets for my wallet, hoping he wasn't about to ask about the weather or tornado warnings.

"Let me tell you something," he volunteered, "never let these guys bully you into rushing."

I looked at him reluctantly.

"The airlines give us all these final boarding calls and make it sound like the world will stop if the plane doesn't leave on time. What they don't tell us is they've been overestimating flight times and expected arrivals for the last decade. They keep all their extra time a secret like they can save up and buy something nice with.

"See here, planes have sat for almost thirty minutes and my flight still says I'll arrive on time." He paused and looked at me expectantly, as if he had just made his point. "The moral of the story is, life is too short to get in a rush."

I nodded automatically and agreeably as I filtered the words through my queasy mind.

"Where ya headed to?" He said, finishing his drink and flagging the bartender for another.

"San Francisco," I didn't want to say.

"Ever been?" the man asked without looking at me.

"No," I replied, almost ending it there but then feeling the uncomfortable itch of sounding rude with a single syllable answer. "You?"

"Just came from there, actually," he boasted. "Between you and me, if California slides into the ocean ..." He shrugged. "No one would miss it but the bill collectors."

I smiled because it reminded me of my dad.

"And I'm a bill collector," he said, laughing to himself.

I watched him receive and thank the bartender for two cups, one with ice and three small bottles of bourbon.

"What is your name?" he asked as he poured one bottle over ice.

"Story," I said, contemplating what drink to order.

"What an interesting name." The corner of his eyebrow perked up. He looked from my face down my body and back to my blushing face. I knew what he was thinking. *What an interesting name for such an uninteresting person.*

"Would you like a drink, Story?" He pushed the first drink toward me.

My mom's voice in my head spouted off irrational fears of taking drinks from strangers, while my dad's voice, perky at the mention of whiskey, told me *one won't hurt.*

"Sure," I said, noticing that he poured the two remaining bottles into the empty cup. *All fire and no ice,* I thought. "What is your name?"

He took a sip along with me before he answered. "Why do I have a feeling you would come up with a much more interesting name for me if I let you?"

I laughed, caught off guard. "What do you mean?"

He shrugged. "You heard me. What name would you pick for me?"

I stuttered, debating his anonymity. Feeling assaulted without any reason to put my finger on. He had dark eyes, framed by long eyelashes and thick eyebrows, like wooly worms that predicted a long, hard winter—black against his dark skin and salt and pepper auburn hair that caught like burning embers in the bar lights.

"Mr. Fox," I finally decided.

He laughed. "Mr. Fox! Mister? You name me an old man and then you name me a clever thief! But I'm such a friendly fellow!"

Blushing, I tried to retract my statement. "I didn't mean anything by it."

"You should mean something by it. Names have power. Don't you know?"

"Well," I said, like words of defense would come but they didn't. We both laughed. "It's just the red hair. It reminded me of a fox. I like foxes. I have never been harmed by a fox. And I read an article about how male foxes make excellent fathers." I stopped speaking upon the realization I was filling the hole I was in, with useless trivia.

"I'm just giving you a hard time." He chuckled and took another sip of his drink. "What do you do, Story?"

"I'm in-between jobs," I lied, trying on a feeling of freedom like it was a coat.

"In-between. In-*between*." He repeated the word as if flipping it over on his tongue and tasting both sides. "At a crossroads?"

I nodded, "You could say that."

"And you're flagging yourself a ride to California?"

"I have a job opportunity there," I tried to lie but felt feverish and cornered.

"But you're not going for that, are you?"

I sipped the bourbon, trying my best to come up with a better answer, but couldn't.

He had a devilish twitch in the corner of his mouth, like a smile or a word that had almost escaped, as if he'd spotted my thoughts peeking through the gap in my lips. His patience was a tangible presence, brushing against my defenses the way wind licks at a wildfire. The burn of the bourbon lingered in my throat. The rest of my confession—the details of what I was running from, the staticky visions of a shapeless future—raced across my tongue and then retreated back into my throat.

"How did you know?" I asked in barely a whisper.

"You have that *dusting-your-broom* aura to you."

I didn't exactly cry, not like I wanted to. Instead, I bit my bottom lip, letting my eyes water. I told him I was sorry.

"What are you apologizing for?" he asked with a gentle laugh.

"I didn't mean to get emotional on you."

"You probably could have lied to me. You just couldn't lie to yourself. Could you?"

I wanted to tell him I lie to myself all the time, but that felt worse somehow. I wanted to tell him that I'm usually an expert crier. I could cry anywhere and probably go unnoticed. I could sob silently. I could use my sleeve just in time to not leave any red swollen evidence. Instead, I said nothing and let the tears fall into my lap.

He extended a handkerchief towards me and said, "It's clean. A fine silk."

I took it from him. The silk was cool to the touch even as it absorbed the tears gathering in the corner of my eyes. He watched me, so I joked, "Too fine for the likes of my tears," but by the time I said it, I realized it wasn't so much a joke but the truth.

"Now what does that mean?"

"It means I'm a piece of shit." I laughed despite myself.

"I don't believe it," he said.

"No, really. I'm a classic case of inherited sin."

"Who needs the devil when you're so quick to condemn yourself?" He shook his head, disapproving.

"What if I told you I didn't even leave a note?" As if this was an unspeakable crime.

"I'd say ..." He paused. "Leaving says a lot on its own." He raised his glass to me. "What if I told you you are exactly where you need to be?"

I played with the handkerchief in my hands, wondering how anyone could possibly know where they were supposed to be. I asked him, "Do you have resources cited to back up your argument?"

He laughed heartily, throwing his head back. "I mean it, Story." And it was at that moment, when I had given him my name and he used it like a thumb tack that pinned me to a cork board. "What is it you really want?"

"I want to runaway," I said.

"You want out."

I nodded.

"Now, why's that?"

"I want to be happy again."

"You were once happy?"

I nodded, "Yeah, when I was younger and didn't mess everything up."

"Ah, so you want to blame this on your youth."

"Well," I said, "I thought I was blaming this on my fucked-up family."

Mr. Fox waved his hands dismissively. "If you were happy, then they were happy, right?"

I considered his words.

He continued, "What do you think it takes to be happy?"

"Making the right decisions?"

"No, no, no." He rolled his eyes. "That's like saying good things happen to good people."

I laughed out loud. "That is, in fact, what people say."

"Don't tell me you believe that mumbo jumbo!"

"Mumbo jumbo?" I laughed. The bourbon was clearly getting to me.

Mr. Fox was readjusting in his seat, his arms flailing, his energy in this conversation rapidly turning turbulent. "What difference does it make if you're making the wrong decision or right decision?"

"I guess you don't believe in heaven?" I asked.

"Look. My beliefs don't make nothin' real." He cleared his throat. "If happiness comes from making the right decisions, how are you gonna tell me which one is right? You do one thing, mess up, and it's *a learning experience*. You do another thing, get it right, and it's too little too late. Then you do another thing, listen to good advice, and somehow, you still get cancer."

I sighed. "Well, how the hell does that help me?"

He laughed. "If something needs changing, what are you willing to do to change it?"

"Anything," I said, automatically.

"Anything?" he asked with his eyebrows perking up.

"Yeah," I said, "probably anything."

"And running away is the best you got?"

I cleared my throat and sipped the bourbon.

"Sure. You can run away. You can believe that paradise is just on the other side of the country. That's fine. And look, I know I'm just an old man. What do I know? But I can say I just came from the other side, and there ain't no paradise there, neither."

"You're saying I should stay here?"

"I ain't sayin' nothing."

"Bullshit," I told him. "You ain't stopped talking since I sat down."

Mr. Fox laughed and nearly fell out of his chair.

"You're right, and I apologize," he finally told me, as he swirled the liquid in his tumbler.

"Okay, but really," I said. "What do you think I should do? Just tell me, and I'll do it."

He raised his eyebrows again. "Oh, now you want me to make the decision?"

"I mean, if there's not a right or wrong decision here..." I said. "Look, I'm tired. I don't know what to do. I know something needs to be done. Just tell me."

"That, Story, is how you lose your soul."

"I don't want a soul," I said, flippantly. "It's damned anyways."

"That easy, huh?" He asked. "To give it all up. Throw the baby out with the bath water. You're so concerned with casting out your demons, you'll cast out the best thing in you."

"Yes," I said because his gaze struck me like lightning. The word tasted like an agreement, the ink of a signature on a contract, slipping through my teeth before I could taste the loss of it.

"Then go, Story," he said, raising a glass. "Dust your broom. Go on. *Git*."

I nodded, raising my glass to him. "Then, it's settled."

"Deal's done," he said.

Our glasses clinked, and I chugged the rest of my bourbon, feeling his words stuck to me, tickling my chest like a stray hair down my shirt. I slammed the glass down like I had something to prove all of a sudden.

I boarded a plane a half hour later. I listened to instructions about exit routes, oxygen masks, and crash positions, while the plane rolled slowly away from the airport. The cabin was silent, as if in collective acknowledgement that something sacred or very dangerous was about to happen. The landscape outside the window was gloomy and wet, broken up only by blinking green lights and red and yellow plastic markers with numbers. The momentum of the take-off pushed me back into my seat. I wanted to fight back but the moment I felt the wheels leave the runway, my body absorbed all the weightlessness from the plane like osmosis, as if I had calculated the correct ratio of speed and inertia. I had burnt enough fuel to propel myself forward, and now, I could sit back and let the jet stream take over.

***

"For a second there," Hunter says, "I thought this was gonna end in a kidnapping."

I laugh.

We stand in the still-hot water, steam billowing up and out the window. Hunter's pack of cigarettes are sitting in the window sill. I want to be the kind of person who smokes in the shower. I pick up the pack and, with my lips, pull out a cigarette.

"What does it mean to dust your broom?" Hunter leans in with his lighter like a gentleman's gentleman.

I suck on the cigarette until the cherry is bright red. "I think it means to leave in a hurry."

"Ah." He nods. "So, just like the blues song."

"Precisely."

"I think Robert Johnson is part of the 27 Club." He says it like it means something. "You know, the famous musicians who didn't live past twenty-seven? Janis Joplin? Jim Morrison?"

I shake my head.

"Kurt Cobain?"

Laughing, I say, "I know the people. I just don't know what the club is."

"They all died at the age of twenty-seven!" Hunter lifts up the black lighter. "And they all had a white lighter in their pocket, which is exactly why I don't use white lighters."

"How old are you?"

"Twenty-six," he says more with his eyebrows than anything else.

"You?"

"I am also 26."

Only the sound of the shower echoes between us as we nod and smoke and then extinguish our cigarettes.

"But I was only twenty-five then," I say.

"So, you didn't have to land in California and immediately find a priest?" He laughs, but I don't.

"Probably should have," I say with a weak smile.

TRACK 5: "GIRL IN THE WAR"

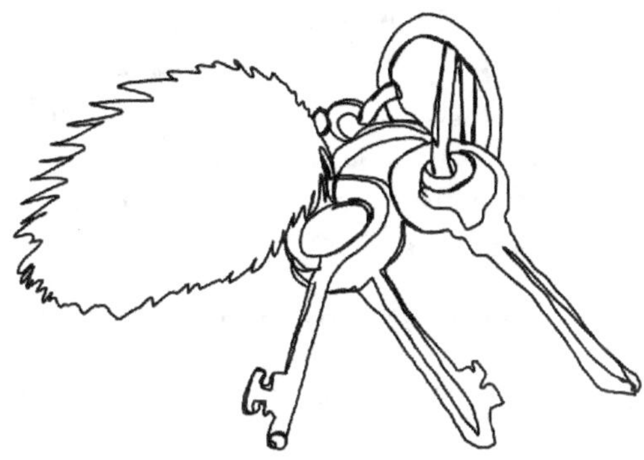

I grew up thinking I was a good luck charm.

My dad called me his little rabbit's foot. He'd take me hunting for arrowheads, ginseng, and morels. He'd have me hold the bucket for his slot machine winnings and pick out the horse at the race track. I was told most of my life that I was lucky—that good things happened when I was around. Whether the forecast called for rain or not, it never rained on me when I didn't want it to, or if it did, it made things better. Like this one time, it barely sprinkled all morning at the theme park and there were no lines. Me and Jodie rode roller coasters one after the other, which is a big deal when you're sixteen years old.

The wedding I photographed in California was a last-minute affair. A family member was being shipped out with the military, and the groom couldn't stand to have his wedding without her. So, they canceled their original date and moved everything forward two months. It was one of those coincidences that felt like good fortune. I was paid upfront with a generous travel fee. They were so thankful for me—the distance I was willing to travel. They said they loved my work, but I'm sure it wouldn't have mattered what I did, how long I was there, or what I wore. Just being there was enough to feel like a hero. It's the easiest way to feel like a saint—to just show up. But they had said more than once that they loved how my photos were so bright and sunny. I didn't explicitly tell them that I was some sort-of lucky charm, but I emphasized that it always seemed to work out.

There wasn't a cloud in sight when my rental car pulled into the parking lot of the restaurant. It had a picturesque view of the Pacific Ocean, beautiful but backwards to me somehow, like I was facing the wrong way on an exit ramp. The couple was standing at the beginning of a path down to the beach. The groom was tall and broad in a well-tailored tux. The bride wore a satin sheath gown, the train of which she held off the ground as her dark, slicked hair caught the sun. I only knew them as Charlie and Ashley.

I extended my hand toward the groom and said, "Charlie?"

"Ashley," he said, as if he'd said it a million times in his lifetime.

Charlie smiled kindly and shook my hand, looking at something over my shoulder.

I turned to find two women approaching us—one older and one that looked related to the groom.

"You guys need to get started right away," the younger one said as she leaned in towards me with her hand on Ashley's shoulder. "Like now."

"The weather forecast says it's going to rain any minute," the older woman added, looking suspiciously at the horizon.

The couple looked at the sky and then me, laughing nervously.

"Hi, I'm Story." I held my hand out to the doomsday guest—there's always one at a wedding.

"Did you hear me?" she asked with a stoney expression.

I dropped my hand and looked at the couple. "I'm ready when

you are."

"Are we ready?" Ashley asked Charlie.

"Where are our flowers?" Charlie asked the doomsday guest.

The younger woman sprinted away but the older woman approached me. She asked me if I'd had a chance to go inside and told me that Charlie had made the centerpieces.

Ashley said they would wait to take photos until they had the flowers, so I followed the older woman toward the restaurant. She told me not to mind Christine and said she was always worried about the time. She introduced herself as Ashley's godmother, and then, as Cecil, her given name when she wasn't being called Momma. She asked if I knew them, and I said no. She explained that they'd been together for over ten years—high school sweethearts even though they'd tried to play it off as if they were just friends. Said she knew they'd end up together. She had been saving to pay for their wedding since they moved in together three years ago. I told her how wonderful that was and she chided me, gently. "If that's what we are calling wonderful these days, then we're all in trouble."

I took great care in photographing six small tables each with large centerpieces: bright blooms in tall glass cylinders filled with trinkets. There were stones, pieces of jewelry, clock hands, buttons, string, swatches of fabric, shark teeth, shells, tiny light bulbs and objects I couldn't identify. I got lost in them as I leaned down and inspected them through the glass. They were like tiny little worlds with strange faces looking back at me from lockets, like friendly neighbors over picket fences.

Christine's screech sliced through the room. "I have the flowers!"

It surprised me. I jolted, and my camera swung forward into the glass cylinder in front of me. It shattered, its contents spreading over the table like a tsunami at a junkyard.

Frozen and heartbroken, I was speechless as it washed over my feet.

"Oh my God," Christine said. "Oh my God." She rushed next to me and tried to cup her hands and gather as many items as she could, like she could scoop them up and protect them, but shards of glass were mixed in. She yelled in pain as blood ran from her hands, mixed with the water, and soaked into the white tablecloths.

Profanities echoed around me. I think she was calling for help, but I was struggling to stand up as I watched everything turn to red. Cecil put a hand on my shoulder and offered me a cup of water. "Everything's fine," she repeated, eyebrows furrowed at the mess—a bio-hazard flooding the restaurant floor.

Just then, Ashley stepped in, his eyes wide and calculating. Christine immediately blamed me, and I let her. It was my fault.

Cecil spoke up. "Everything's fine. We've got it. Keep Charlie out there."

Ashley nodded but then said, "The thing is, we've got another problem. The bouquet is wrong, they must have gotten mixed up at the florists."

"What?" Christine, still struggling to stop the bleeding from her hands, exclaimed. "They had your name on them!"

Then the groom looked at me. "Do we have time to run back to the florist?"

Centerpiece tragedy aside, I wanted to tell him I didn't know. I don't know when photographers became event planners, time keepers, traffic reporters, weather forecasters, farmer almanac writers, interior designers, or light technicians. We can't control the weather any more than we can control time and space. I always felt like I was being confused for Einstein every time a client asked me whether they had time to do something. *It's relative,* I wanted to say. *What are the variables? How many miles away is the florist? How many traffic lights are there? What's the top speed on your '95 Subaru? Will rain slow you down? If it rains while you're gone, you have until it stops raining. Actually, let me check the sunset times, because, really, I just need the thirty minutes before sunset and I can make it look like we had hours.*

But I didn't say any of that. Instead, I told him he had time. Couples don't want to be overwhelmed with variables and options and doomsday guests talking about weathermen who, at best, guess for a living, and at worst, lie. They wanted to hear *Yes* and *We'll make it work.* And people do make it work, because weddings hold a special place in everyone's hearts. They are the festivals of a tribe. They are the exception to the rules. They are holidays, and cheat days, and holy days, and what-happens-in-Vegas-stays-in-Vegas days. Things have always worked out for me as their photographer, because there's always a village of people whose ears perk and spines straighten at the opportunity to do anything for a person in a white wedding dress.

But I was wrong. I was wrong when I said they'd have time. Large black clouds moved in as soon as they left. The rain hit, hard as ever, as soon as they got back. Ashley did tell Charlie about the broken centerpiece, so before her wedding, she tried to salvage the wreckage. I told them we'd have time after the ceremony to take photos once the rain stopped.

For the most part, the ceremony went off without a hitch. It was a short and sweet thing, officiated by the sister in her dress blues. It rained and thundered throughout the ceremony. As the couple kissed, the restaurant lost power, shrouding them in darkness save for the candles along the windows that Cecil had thought to light. The photo of the first kiss was just a silhouette of the bride and groom against those candles with storm clouds barely visible beyond the windows.

The power never came back on, and the rain never stopped. The restaurant brought out more candles. The food was kept warm with chafing dishes. All the guests walked around with candles like we were at mass, like we were mourning the loss of everything the day could have been.

All weddings are held together by bare threads and crossed fingers. I've repaired zippers and taped tits into strapless gowns. I've spot-cleaned wine, ketchup, and baby diarrhea from maid-of-honor dresses. I've seen tuxedos catch on fire and gold-flake covered cakes melt in the sun. I've seen bridesmaids pass out during the ceremony and be kicked out of the venue during the reception. It's an odds game. Ninety percent of your day will be great regardless of what goes wrong. Ten percent of your day will be fucked. When it's all over, you'll laugh about it like it was just a weird little quirk. *You remember when your dad got drunk? Remember when the best man was late because his car got towed?* For this wedding, however, the ratio was off. Even the air in the restaurant was tired of holding the tension. Logically, I knew

I couldn't affect the weather, but it sure felt like I had brought nothing but bad luck to the day.

After dinner, they cut the cake. Instead of feeding each other, they cut a piece for each guest, handing them out reverently. As everyone ate cake, Christine stood up and tapped on her glass to make a toast.

She said, "Not one thing has gone right today." She looked from the guests to the couple. "Not one." They smiled back and forth, and then she continued. "It's so dark in here, I've missed my mouth trying to feed myself cake. I guess you can't have the cake and eat it too." Polite laughter followed, but her face grew serious. "That's the thing about marriage. We don't have any way of preparing for the storm that threatens it. It sneaks up from behind the treetops while we are admiring the horizon. We think we have time to enjoy the shifting colors of the sunset and the wind on our face and that it will never go away or change directions. But the storms do come, and they hit hard and fast, and they don't take prisoners." She didn't blink as she scanned the quiet room. Only the *pitter-patter* of rain on the windows could be heard between her words. "The only way out is through. You never give up, you never back down, and you cling to each other when everything feels insurmountable. As Ashley and Charlie proved today and every day, nothing is insurmountable." Finally, she looked at the groom whose head rested against the bride's head. His lips were pressed against her temple. "I know these two," Christine continued. "They are like fighters born to lose but never give up. And when they eat their cake, they'll share it too."

The room erupted in applause. The restaurant filled with the kind of joy that was felt more than seen. It moved everyone to tears, Cecil worst of all. The room flickered with candlelight, smiles, and flashes of lightning, but it was no competition against the collective magic of their village of supporters and loved ones who rooted for them and celebrated their win.

I felt like the elephant in the room. I could feel everyone's fingers twitching and itching to point at me. Like I was just another obstacle this couple had to overcome. I was the storm they didn't see coming. The storm that raged around them outside the kingdom's gates. But in retrospect, no one paid attention to me. I was inconsequential. I was a fly on the wall—a ghost in the shadows. I documented moments like a paparazzi, feeling both like I didn't belong and like nothing I did could capture the real beauty of these fighters.

The oil painter they had hired would put me to shame. He presented his work to the couple as they said goodbye to their last guest. I was able to capture the bride and groom in tears marveling at the work before I laid my own eyes on it.

He had captured it.

He captured that thing evading me—that thing that was slipping between my fingers every time I clicked the shutter. While I was hunting for it in the candlelight on the guest's faces, he had found it in the shadows around them, like a Rembrandt painting of the prodigal son. Only after seeing his careful application of subtle shades of purple and gold did I realize the darkness was just as important as the light.

***

"That made me hungry," Hunter said, rubbing his belly. And when I didn't say anything, he cleared his throat. "Not to downplay how stressful that must have been. Weddings are such a to-do, you know?"

I laugh. "Yeah, I know."

"Would you want all that?" Hunter asks me, as his head is submerged in the showerhead and his hair falls in plump rivulets.

"Want what?" I ask while drawing the waves of an ocean in the fog on the window.

"The wedding stuff? The cake and photographers," he says, not opening his eyes.

I shrug even though he can't see me. "I don't think marriage is for me."

"Me neither," he says as he leans out of the stream of water and wipes his eyes.

I nod absentmindedly, staring back at my foggy landscape.

"So, when do I come into the story?" he asks.

52

TRACK 6: "FISH STICKS"

You were the carrot that the universe dangled in front of me—the prize that I knew was out of reach but I went for it anyway.

Before we met, earlier that day, I went to a job interview for some part-time gig that paid barely over $10. I thought if I could get a job, I would stay in California and never go home. The job advertised a *fast-paced environment* and a *goal-oriented workforce*. I applied online and got a call back within a couple days.

I thought I was a shoe-in.

All my life I'd worked hard to exceed expectations. I'd arrived early, stayed late, done the bonus work, won awards, and gone above and beyond for clients. My resume was short, but the reviews online were not—they were lengthy and glowing. What showed motivation and ambition like building your own company and wearing all the hats?

I showed up early to the interview, dressed like I cared about making an impression. I was witty with my small talk, making the hiring manager laugh. He'd printed out my application and complimented me on my communication skills. He asked what I went to college for. I told him I got a liberal arts degree, because it was easier than explaining the truth. I hadn't been able to decide between art history, religion, and psychology, so I'd done them all, and that's what they'd labeled it.

He bounced in his swivel chair, leaning on his elbow with his finger on his chin. "And what have you done in the five years since college?"

I said, "I've built an award-winning business from the ground up."

"I see," he said. "So, you've really only worked for yourself?"

"I work for my clients," I said. "I spend, on average, a year with each of them, building trust and communicating goals that we accomplish together in one action packed day."

"Yes," he said, as though I'd missed the point. "But you've never worked in a team setting under the direction of a supervisor?"

I caught myself before saying my spiel about weddings being one big team rooting for couples. I started to suspect that he wanted me to admit that I'd never had a boss. I got the sense that it was important to him that I had experience being subservient to someone else.

He spoke before I could think of a response. "Look. You've obviously worked very hard and accomplished a lot. I congratulate you on a job well done. However, I'm worried that you won't make a good fit with our team. We need team players. I'm looking to hire someone with more experience in the restaurant industry. It's a different beast than working for yourself. You have to look out for customers and your co-workers, and I'm just not sure. I want to be sure. You know?"

He was bouncing and spinning in his chair, looking at my application like everything was written right there in black and white. He just didn't know how to get me to see it.

I started to speak, but he interrupted me.

"What if you focus on beefing up your resume. Get some experience, on a team and under a supervisor. Collect some references from that experience and come back to me."

Finally, he dropped his hand and my application on the desk in front of him. He leaned forward. The creak of his chair was long and drawn out, like a door slowly closing.

"You want me," I said, finger pointing to myself, "to go out and get a job." I pointed to his office window. "So that I can come back and get a job?" I pointed to his desk.

His smile was false. He was done with me. "Be humble," he said. "Start from the bottom just like everybody else."

"The bottom? This is the bottom. I'm taking a pay cut to work for you. I'm stepping down. I'm—" I was done with him. I stood up abruptly. "The job is for a fucking door greeter. You could put a cardboard cutout of a bear in a bandana and a *free selfies* T-shirt at the door, and no one would give a fuck."

It was petty and probably proved his point, but I was on edge. Everything felt like an attack on my decision to leave Kentucky—the wedding, the interview, the man from the airport. I stormed out.

I called Jodie, who maybe would have been on my side but was too offended herself.

"I'm glad you didn't get the job," Jodie said. "That's what you get for leaving and not even saying goodbye. What a bitch."

"Nothing is set in stone. I'm not choosing homelessness over returning home." I stopped and caught my breath. "It was a pipe dream. I thought it would be easy. I thought I could just drop everything and make it happen."

Jodie sighed. "I get it. You've been in a bit of a funk for a while."

We were both silent. A Subaru flew past me up the hill and ran a red light.

"Look. I admire your spontaneity. Like, damn, girl, go get 'em." Jodie laughed. " But if I may offer a suggestion, maybe scale back the energy a bit. You know? Start with, like, a haircut or a new car. Or, damn, if you're that hard up, go to a bar, find a stranger to go home with, wear a condom, get it out of your system, and then come back home."

Blood pulsed in my ears and in my feet. The sun was nearly setting and it was still so early. The city was truly golden, and even though I couldn't see the bay or the bridge from where I was, I could see the magic of the city like a gate wide open and waiting for me to walk through it.

"Okay," I told Jodie. "Okay."

She laughed and asked, "Okay?"

"Yeah," I said. "I'm going to get drunk and have a one-night stand. I'm going to sleep with a stranger tonight."

I hung up before she or I could pretend it was just a joke. I was on a main road. I could look up a map but wanted to see what would happen if I took the next right. I didn't want to know what I could find. I wanted to know what could find me.

A large purple octopus found me. Its painted tentacles reached out from a brick wall and corralled me into a long narrow bar. I tied the corners of my dress shirt in a knot above my belly button, like it would make me look more female, but I still waited in line for a beer. I found a space to stand on the side wall with my back to velvet, watching a band get ready on stage.

Then, I saw you.

You were with Frankie. You both squeezed through the crowd and stood in front of me. You not only looked out of place, you also looked out of time. Your hair was slicked back like a fifties greaser. In the dim light, you looked like you might be on a Camel Lights billboard, making smoking look cool for all the unsuspecting youth.

No one on stage wore any shoes, and there were no instruments. There were only wood saws, deer antlers, and bells. Finally, a man in a moth-eaten T-shirt and ragged mid-calf jeans approached a microphone and spoke to the crowd. He welcomed us, gestured to the floor, and told the crowd to feel free to take off our shoes and sit for the show. About half of the crowd sat, looking like a kindergarten class preparing for story time. They proceeded with what I can only describe as a bastardized ritual or psychedelic trip performance.

You and your friend were laughing, drawing attention from the patrons around you. I wasn't surprised when you guys left, squeezing past me. I remember thinking *what kind of person has the confidence to leave before the end of the show?*

I smelled cigarettes as you passed, so I followed you out a few seconds later.

I didn't even have to look for you outside. I would have been drawn to you even if my eyes had been closed. You were standing and smoking outside, under the glow of the streetlights. You looked like Marlon Brando with cigarette smoke twisting up from your smirk and a soft cotton shirt beneath your leather jacket. A few greasy locks of hair fell forward over your forehead towards your eyebrows—thick, dark, and slightly unkempt. I'd never been so jealous of a cigarette as I watched you take a drag with your full lips, plump and—

You noticed me watching you.

I patted my shirt and dress pants as if looking for cigarettes. You watched me approach you, like you weren't sure whether I was going to walk right past. I wasn't sure myself.

Frankie held out a hand to stop me. He introduced himself and said, "Excuse me. Do you have a moment to answer an important question?"

He sounded like a Mormon, like he was about to ask about the state of my soul. I nodded, eyeing the cigarette in your mouth.

Frankie asked me, "Were you inside? At the show?"

I nodded.

"Okay," he said. "Would you sleep with any of those men on stage?"

I asked you for a cigarette and said I'd need a moment to think about it.

"If that's not deflecting the question, I don't know what is,"

Frankie whispered to you, about me.

I didn't even defend myself.

You watched me with your head tilted. The smoke from your lungs created a smoke screen. You became more mysterious by the minute.

"Depends on how desperate I was. How long it had been. You know?"

"How desperate?" Frankie pointed at me. "What do you know about desperation?"

I coughed out an *excuse me?*

He rolled his eyes at me. "Women can get sex whenever they want." Then, he looked me up and down and stepped back. "Wait." I recognized the look he gave me. He saw my flat chest, more pubescent boy than adult woman, and my dirty shoulder-length hair, more Hanson's brother than Gwen Stefani. He didn't know what gender I was.

I twisted my head and raised an eyebrow. "What?" I asked, enjoying how uncomfortable he was.

"Shit," was all he said. He dropped his hands in surrender. "I don't know how to fix this."

I genuinely laughed and so did you.

"That's not true," I proclaimed, leaving all other questions unanswered. "Women struggle plenty. Because men don't know where anything is."

"Hi." He stepped toward me with a hand out. "My name is Frankie, and I know where all the good spots are."

"I've heard that so many times," I said, shaking my head.

Frankie smiled at you and stepped back. "But back to the original issue. Women hold the power. They have the fucking fruit from the tree of good and evil in their goddamn hands. Men will do whatever they want. Who was it who said that?"

You shook your head.

"You know, something like, women rule the world. No man has ever done anything that a woman either hasn't allowed him to do."

"Oh, Dylan," you said.

"Yes, Dylan!"

No one had explicitly mentioned Eve's name, but it got me thinking about sin and how she fucked it up for everyone. She knotted the ropes. You can't even blame the serpent. The Devil just told her what she already knew—that she wanted a taste of that fucking apple.

"It's true," you added. Your eyes were penetrating, like you were affirming my thoughts.

"So, if a woman approached you tonight," I asked Frankie, "and wanted to have sex, you'd say yes? No questions?"

He nodded emphatically. I turned the question onto you.

"Hell, yes he would," Frankie said for you.

"You'd say yes?" I asked you again, needing to hear your answer.

You nodded at me, throwing your cigarette butt down on the pavement like that was your opinion of Paradise.

I winked at you.

Frankie rolled his eyes with his whole body, somehow. "Of course, you get the wink." He stepped between us. "See, herein lies the problem. If we want to have sex tonight and we ask a woman, she's going to say no. I mean, individually, not both of us together. But, hell, if she said yes, we'd probably still go for it." He took a moment to shake the image of a threesome from his mind. "But women don't ask us." He gestures madly toward the stage beyond the octopus mural. "Not when they can sleep with the bay area's ayahuasca leader, who, I would bet my last cigarette, is going to howl when he climaxes."

"And the howling offends you?" I asked nonchalantly.

He looked so defeated. "Yes, I suppose it does."

You said the howling didn't bother you.

I said, "If there's no howling, I'm disappointed."

Frankie didn't laugh but you did. You looked at me like I surprised you. I liked surprising you.

You waited until then to introduce yourself.

When I told you my name, you moved right on to your next question, like you couldn't gather enough information at once.

"Tell me your all-time favorite song."

I said, "Impossible."

"Artist?"

I asked, "Seriously?"

"Who's the first band to come to mind?"

"Limp Bizkit."

You laughed out loud, drawing attention from strangers.

You said you were hungry.

I said I wasn't.

Then you asked me, "Have you eaten anything since the forbidden fruit, or does that stuff last a while?" You leaned in and your breath was warm. "Or is it more like a chip? The hunger never ends." Then you asked me what I wanted to eat more than anything in the world.

I leaned into you like I was going to kiss you right there, in front of a bored Frankie and a giant purple octopus, and I said "fish sticks."

***

Hunter is laughing, "I remember the night differently."

"Oh, yeah? So, now, I'm a bad storyteller?"

"No, you just make me sound so cool and collected. The truth is I was a nervous wreck. You make it sound like I strolled into that venue and waltzed out too cool for school."

"Too cool for school?" I laughed. "Who says that?"

"I saw you in the venue, against the wall." Hunter says, "I smelled you too. You were intoxicating." His eyes are dreamy as he says it, and if it weren't for the glazed look in his eyes, I wouldn't have believed him. "I didn't leave because the music was bad. I left because I didn't want to be the kind of creep who just turned around and kissed you. I have never wanted to accidentally spill a drink on someone before just to have an immediate excuse to face them—touch them."

"You're lying," I say.

He shakes his head. "Then, you found us outside. I don't remember Frankie babbling. I must have tuned it out. I just remember thinking I felt like a crazy person. Or maybe I was drugged. I couldn't form words. I thought, *is this what a seizure feels like?* I thought you would write me off as some awkward, shy man. And then I thought, *wait, she followed me.*

"And when you said fish sticks, I thought of the song by The Heligoats and how I don't understand the lyrics, but I still play it on repeat." He smiles as he approaches me, like he's going to kiss me. Instead, he searches my face, perhaps for something from that night.

I'm leaning against the wall of the shower, out of the water. My skin is shriveling on my fingertips, and I think the water can't stay warm for much longer or I'll become a water-logged corpse.

"How much do you remember from that night?" I ask him, shifting out of his gaze nervously.

"I remember drinking too much. I remember your driving. I remember being in the back of the van best of all."

I blush. "So, you remember waking up?"

"Yes," he says with a long exhale. "You were gone, and I thought you had been a dream."

TRACK 7: "GOD DON'T MAKE LONELY GIRLS"

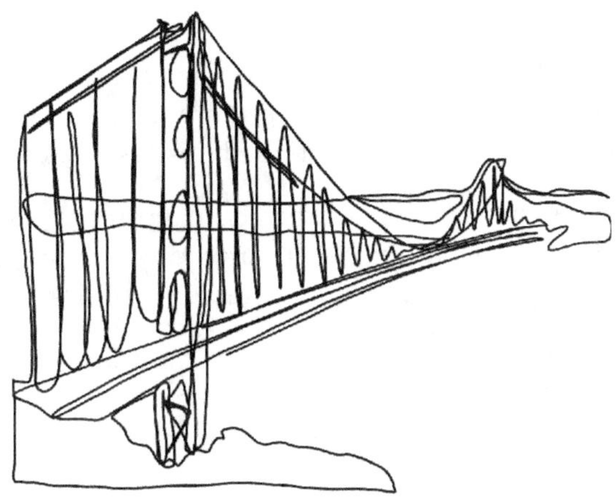

You let me drive. You sat up front with me, while Frankie sat in the back on the edge of a mattress with his elbow on the side of your headrest. You navigated, pointing the way around Fisherman's Wharf, looking for actual, honest-to-God fish sticks.

We found a food truck that was walk-up only. Its sign said *Late Night Food*. I was gonna get out but you told me to drive up on the sidewalk and pull up to the counter like it was a drive through. I scraped the side of your van's roof on the awning and you never yelled or got mad at me. You just looked at the roof like *that was a weird noise,* and then, you leaned over me and out the driver's side window.

"Ya'll got any fish sticks hot 'n' ready?" You asked it in your best country accent.

The vendor was so shocked it took a few minutes for them to register what was happening. The poor man just shook his head no.

You asked, "What about some ketchup?"

The vendor pointed towards a tray at the end of the counter.

"Story, can you be so kind as to get me to the Ketchup."

I pressed my foot down and the van lurched forward. You grabbed a big handful of ketchup packets. Then, you saluted the vendor as I eased away from the food truck, putting on my turn signal and dismounting the sidewalk to merge back in with traffic. Frankie thought it was hilarious.

I don't remember who pulled a fifth of whiskey out, but it was like fuel to the fire. We tried three more restaurants. I parked in the street with the hazards on while you questioned hostesses about their menu.

We ended up at Target. I parked the van on the top floor of the parking garage and we rode the elevator down into the store. The Wallflowers were playing. You and Frankie were singing under your breath on either side of me.

"I guess you guys like this song?" I asked.

"Such a good song," you said.

I loved the way you said it, though. The long guttural vowel, pushed to its limit, rang through me. I started when the elevator doors dinged open.

We exited the elevator and navigated to the grocery section.

"That song was on every mix CD I made for at least a year," you said. Then, you asked me, "Did you ever burn CDs when you were a kid?"

"Of course," I told you. "That was the '90s kids' love language."

"It was, wasn't it?" You smiled.

"Do you remember any of the titles you gave them?" I asked.

"Remember?" Frankie said over his shoulder at us. "He still has them all."

I pictured dozens of rewritable CDs abandoned on the dashboard and ruined by the greenhouse effect, just like they warned us about the VHS rentals from Blockbuster. "They survived?"

"Debatable," you said. There was one you still had, because you were quite proud of it. It was a break-up playlist for a girlfriend. You had titled it *Only Violent Roses are Red*.

In the frozen food aisle, Frankie pointed toward some value-brand fish sticks. I read the back of the box. I asked if anyone had a plan for heating them up.

You winked at me and paid for the fish sticks. I thought, *is this supposed to be sexy? Are fish sticks code for something? Was I willing to play it cool and play along?*

While walking to the van, you asked me, "What about you? What was your favorite burned CD title?"

I told you about a mix CD that a boy in college made for me titled *Rainbow Bright*. "There was … 'Holland, 1945' by Neutral Milk Hotel, … 'Girl Anachronism' by Dresden Dolls, and … 'Every Man Needs a Molly' by Say Anything."

"Did it work?" Frankie asked me as we piled back into your van.

"Did what work?"

"Did he get into your pants?"

"No." I shook my head. "But it was still a good playlist. Better than the playlist I made him."

"He made you a CD, and you made him a CD, but you didn't sleep with him?" Frankie spun around.

"I don't owe anyone anything," I said quickly.

He glanced at you.

Maybe it was just me, but I thought I could sense your preemptive disappointment. I could feel the bets placed on me. Everything the night had been so far didn't change the fact that it could all go sideways. One of us could still lose it all.

What I didn't say was that I loved that boy. I loved that he called me Rainbow Bright despite those years being my darkest. His mix CD didn't get abandoned or damaged. It was played until I recognized that it couldn't be played anymore. Then, I stowed it away like a secret. I was ashamed that I treated it like a wedding vow never professed. I remember hanging out with him, and I, like a jackass, would tell him, "You know this isn't a date, right?" I don't know why I did that. I don't know why I wouldn't let myself have him. I'd always go back to the guys who were bad for me—just like a stereotype or a record needle bouncing on that last groove, repeating the last chords.

Sporadically, we would call each other, one or both of us, maybe a little toasted. We'd talk like it would end up *us against the world*—like it was inevitable, and we just had to bide our time.

It was all I could do not to look back and remind myself, *yep, that is where I fucked up.*

But now, I didn't think there was another option. It had been a rite of passage. The nickname was a technicolor dream coat. I messed that up, and I'd mess up again. It was best not to place your bets on me.

But this wasn't the kind of thing someone said over fish sticks.

"Must not have been the best playlist." Frankie said, patting you on the shoulders. "Now here is a man who can make a playlist."

I asked him what that meant as I navigated out of the parking garage.

"Hunter here is a radio DJ. He just finished a three-day guest spot on the local college radio station this week. We were supposed to be celebrating tonight."

He was being such a good wingman and all you could focus on was getting me to a Chevron gas station. As I put the van in park, you snatched the fish sticks from the floorboard and disappeared inside, leaving me with Frankie in the van.

I asked him if you guys lived in San Francisco.

He told me, he did but that you were just visiting.

I could see the top of your head over the top of the chip aisle. You were against the back wall, using the gas station's microwave. Frankie was lying back on the mattress, possibly a little drunk. When I noticed the mattress was covered in clothes and food wrappers and empty cigarette packs I asked Frankie if you lived out of your van.

Frankie laughed at me. Told me not to worry. That you'd take me to a hotel if my standards were higher.

Frankie's call out on my intentions was unsettling, like he recognized a predator.

I was sweating as you walked out of the Chevron. You were smiling. The gas-pump illuminated you in a greenish-white light, like you were an aged oil painting of the last supper. The steaming orange fish sticks on a paper plate were the eucharist.

You handed them to me through the van window, pulled out a new pack of cigarettes from your jacket pocket, and tossed them into my lap. *Take, eat; this is my body which is broken for you: this do in remembrance of Me.*

"Drop me off before you two head off into the sunset," Frankie said from the back of the van.

You nodded and acted like it was part of the plan, like it was perfectly normal for some stranger to replace your friend at some point in the night. I figured you did this all the time. That this was a mutual agreement. That I accepted burned CDs and didn't put out, and you picked up women who were fine with a one-night stand in a van. I convinced myself no harm would be done as I ate the fish sticks irreverently.

I was licking my fingers when you asked me how they were. I thought about telling you that they tasted like sin—greasy, savory, and mouth-watering. Instead, I told you they were a little cold in the middle, like a subliminal warning for the upcoming letdown.

When we dropped Frankie off, I asked you, "I guess you're sleeping in here tonight?"

"Depends," you said, leaning away from me in your seat with your shoulder against the passenger door. You asked me if I planned on sleeping in the van. You didn't even ask if I had a hotel. I did, by the way.

I looked back at the mattress and saw the windows in the back with their curtains drawn. I asked you to find us a place with a view, and I would sleep in the van.

You got me to the park-and-ride across the Golden Gate Bridge. I didn't tell you then, but that was the first time I'd seen the bridge. The whole time I drove, I couldn't stop thinking about how the bridge is more famous for suicide than for anything else.

After parking so that the back doors to your van opened up to a view of San Francisco, we drank the rest of Frankie's whiskey. I asked you where you were from, and when you said Kentucky, I couldn't believe it. One minute, I'd been driving across a bridge, believing the world was large enough to stretch out in. The next minute, the world becomes so small I thought I'd been committed and locked in a padded room. I panicked. I lied. I told you I was from Kansas, as if a tornado had picked me up and dropped me off at your van.

We smoked all our cigarettes, even the stale ones from your glove box, listening to music on some app on your phone. I asked about the tattoo on your hand and you played a song for me about a self-destructive girl who never put out. You said you thought it was inspirational but I couldn't stop thinking how we were playing the parts and how much I wanted to change the ending.

When you asked me if I had a tattoo, I shrugged like I wanted you to find it for yourself. You just laughed and didn't move any closer. You said your mom was furious when you got yours. She said you had ruined your future and any prospect of a good job. You said she had asked you point blank, "What are you going to say when you're questioned at the golden gates?" I knew you meant heaven but I was looking at the bridge thinking of all the people who didn't know the answer to the question and jumped anyway. Perhaps it was why they jumped.

When your phone died, you asked for my phone so you could play a Bob Dylan song. I had forgotten about the background image on my phone and you asked me who was in the photo. I told you it was the local weatherman—a celebrity encounter.

"Oh, yeah," you said, "I sort of hate that guy."

As I laughed too hard for it to make any sense, you downloaded the app on my phone, logged into your account, and kept playing songs like all you wanted to do was listen to them with me.

When our hands no longer had cigarettes and whiskey bottles to distract them, we finally sat in silence. We stared at San Francisco as it blinked back at us. Your knee brushed my knee. The cool bay air curled around us, shaping us both into a half circle, not quite whole.

I kissed you.

I kissed you like I had you trapped.

I whispered, into your ear, a line from one of the songs you played me.

You whispered it back.

***

I am holding myself because the water has finally lost its heat.

Hunter turns it off. I'm surprised he hasn't said anything yet. I can't figure out what that means. I wonder if he regrets that night as I grab two towels from the hooks on the wall. I take Jodie's and give him mine. The bathroom is steamy and hot like a sauna. And yet I am cold and I don't think I will ever warm up. I am scaly like a dragon with the goosebumps that are forming on my skin.

"I figured out you were from Kentucky," he finally says, patting his naked body "when I recognized the weatherman on your phone. I thought maybe you didn't claim Kentucky. It didn't matter to me. I just didn't want the night to end. Like, the wanting was the best part. Like, if I could stretch out the night, I'd bend some space-time continuum, and not even the sunrise could ruin it."

"And then the sex ruined it?" I ask, trying to sound like I'm joking.

"And then you *leaving* ruined it," he says.

"Sorry about that."

He is drying off his face when he asks, "How did you leave? How did you get home? Or wherever you were staying?"

"I walked across the bridge," I say.

"Christ, how far is that?"

"Far enough to regret," I say with a weak laugh. "I took public transit when I got to the other side, but it was still a very long walk."

"Why didn't you stay?"

I take a big breath and force myself to look at him, so that I can gauge any emotion on his face and make it my own, like a penance due. "Because I woke up to a text from my husband. The man in the background photo on my phone. The man who gave me the rings I was hiding in my pants pocket. After working nonstop, he had finally started to wonder where I was."

TRACK 8: "DESPERADOS UNDER THE EAVES"

My mother had betrayed me.

Seventy tornadoes had been confirmed. Forty-one people had died. Five inches of snow fell three days later. My husband had been busy with work. When he realized he was too exhausted to drive home, he had called me for a ride. When he called my mom wondering where I was, she tore him a new one, said family should come first, no matter what your job was.

Which is rich coming from the person who told him where I was hiding. All of us were passing around guilt like a hot potato.

My husband was the first to apologize. He begged me to come home. I told him I would; I just needed time. I said it like he deserved to hold the guilt, as if I hadn't been the runaway, as if I hadn't just slept with you on a mattress in the back of an Astro van.

I was so exhausted from the walk, the public transit, and the phone calls. For two days, I recovered by drinking in my two-star sea-side motel room. When I wasn't listening to music on the app you put on my phone, I was listening to the air conditioner hum. I didn't want to go home and be the prodigal son, but I didn't deserve to stay and find happiness. I sure as hell didn't deserve you. I couldn't live with myself. Every direction felt like the wrong one.

When I checked into my hotel before the wedding, it was a dingy tan and white, an outdated attempt at neutral and classy. Within a week, a painters' crew had painted it vibrant orange and blue. I finally emerged from the hotel on the third day, thinking I was a new person in a new place.

I decided I would get a tattoo. I picked out a place that was open late. When I walked in, the artist told me to wait. It was then that I noticed the parlor walls were covered in portraits of the savior. I looked around and wondered, *did I just walk into a church? A tattoo parlor operated by a church?*

The tattoo artist returned and introduced herself as Anna.

I told her I wanted a scarlet letter.

"That's a terrible idea," she said. "Why in the hell would you do that?"

I wanted to memorialize a mistake, so that history didn't repeat itself.

Anna seemed to believe that was only a good idea for world wars.

I was nervous. I couldn't even do tattoos right. Once again, I was directionless. I stood in the eyes of god, playing with my car keys, wishing I could smoke cigarette after cigarette. Anna noticed the knotted rope and asked about it.

"Oh, this is just a family mantra of sorts. It means, *when you get to the end of your rope, tie a knot in it, and hang on.*"

She asked me if I read Tarot and she started sketching. She said, "There's this one card, the three of swords. It's sort of like this." Then she pointed out a specific painting of Christ. One hand opened his robe to reveal his thorn wrapped and bleeding heart and another hand held his fingers crossed, like for good luck. The portrait was gilded and his tortured heart was vibrant candy red, and yet his eyes reminded me of a puppy. Like he had learned one thing in his history of dealing with humans, and it was this: if I look like a puppy, they will do what I want.

Anna finished the sketch and showed me. There was a knot of ropes shaped like a human heart, as if anatomically correct. The aorta was the frazzled end of one rope. The veins and arteries were smaller ropes tangled up with it. There were three swords pierced through it.

"Can you make it really peppy, like this guy?" I pointed to the gilded Christ with the bleeding heart. If he was holding out for good luck, then I could too.

I decided I needed it on my rib cage. She tried to warn me against it. She said it was the most painful place I could put it.

Every holy gaze was on me, asking me if I deserved any less pain. So, I insisted she put it on my ribs.

The moment the needle touched my skin, I knew I had grossly underestimated the level of pain I had committed to. After two hours, I thought I might resort to violence towards Anna. Another artist had come in since we'd started. She just stood there. She had long dark hair and her arms and legs were covered in ink. I couldn't believe she was watching me in agony and doing nothing to save me.

"Almost finished," Anna said, but I didn't believe her. She'd said it before, and it was obvious we had different ideas of what the word almost meant.

She wiped a wet paper towel over my ribcage. It felt like sandpaper, or wet shoe laces, or nails on a chalkboard, or brooms on carpet, if those things were translated into a physical sensation.

"I can't believe I have friends who have told me this wouldn't hurt," I said quickly, in effort to not scream the words through gritted teeth.

"It's like I should have warned you or something." Anna laughed to herself.

"Yeah," the other girl said with her mouth full of a candy bar. "This is pretty ambitious for a first tattoo. I just figured you were a glutton for punishment."

"It's pretty badass, actually." Anna nodded at me in our reflection in a wall-length mirror facing me.

I nodded back with my teeth grinding too much to smile.

"It looks good." The other girl leaned over Anna's shoulder. I could only see the very edge of the tattoo in the mirror but was avoiding looking at the needle for fear I would pass out.

"So, what brings you to California? Vacation?" Anna asked me.

Maybe my mind was tricked into thinking I was being tortured for information, but all of my secrets just sort of spilled out of me, as if their release would stop the pain. "I wish I was on vacation," I confessed, "but actually, I tried to run away."

Anna's needle hesitated, and started again.

"I met a guy that I really liked … and slept with him," I said. "Which means I cheated on my husband."

I had lain there for more than two hours, practically topless, and now I was holding nothing back.

"And my mother tattletale-ed on me."

I laughed and it hurt. Anna's needle paused.

"Now, I'm going back because, well, I don't know what else to do."

Anna's needle returned to a spot fresh meat.

"Maybe I am a glutton for punishment," I said with my eyes tightly closed.

"Shit. That's a lot." Anna's needle mercifully pulled away again.

"The only way out is through," the other girl said, several seconds later.

Anna laughed. "What are you talking about?"

"That's a thing they say," the girl said defensively.

"A thing who says about what?"

"You know, about hardships like marriage and whatnot," the girl explained.

We were all silent until out of nowhere, Anna yelled, "What the fuck does that mean?"

"You know," the girl shifted around to Anna's other side. "Well, I don't know. That's just what they say. Like you can't go around it. You can't go back. You just have to go through." She held her hands flat against each other and sliced the air. "Like trying to cross a river, or a mountain. Although, obviously you could go around a mountain. And you could get a boat. You don't have to swim. You could get creative. But yeah, you have to go through somehow."

Anna stared at her, bewildered. I soaked up every second of not being stabbed repeatedly.

Their laughter filled the room.

"That's your last idiom today. You've met your quota."

"I thought you loved my idioms!"

"I do, but that doesn't mean you can force them onto unsuspecting customers."

They both looked at me in the mirror. I smiled weakly and without any social grace asked, "Is it done?"

"It is done," Anna said, even as she wiped the ink over and over, looking at the fresh tattoo, tilting her head side to side. "Yes, finito. Go check it out in the mirror and tell me what you think."

My body, cold and stiff, rolled off the padded bench like a corpse raised from the dead. I pressed my bundled T-shirt against my chest, rotated and raised my arm, and looked over my shoulder at myself in the mirror.

Bright and piercing primary colors were accented by bold black lines with hints of both real and inked blood seeping from between the knots—between the gaps in my rib cage.

Anna and the other girl joined me in front of the mirror. As I stood, they bent over. Their noses were inches from my body—my ribs and my blood—as if we were in a Caravaggio painting. Anna's gloved hands touched me gently as she said, "It's pretty swollen."

The other girl pointed along the lines, "The contrast is so striking. Your shadow work makes the colors pop off her skin. Beautiful."

"Oh, wow," Anna said with her eyes widened at my ribcage.

"What?" I asked.

"I think I can see your heartbeat."

The girl laughed, like she didn't believe Anna, and leaned in closer. Then, her face sobered.

I could feel my pulse in my palms, my feet, and my crown. I had no doubt my blood was rushing through every vein in my body.

"What do you think?" Anna asked, glancing toward me.

"I think it was worth the pain," I said, mostly meaning it. The tattoo felt like a battle wound, a scar I had earned, a shield I could carry forward, and a knot in a rope keeping me from falling away.

I found the portrait on the wall behind me, the one I had asked to imitate. Christ looked back at me with his fingers crossed. I swear his large eyes were on my rib cage. His head inclined toward me, and he was frowning. I realized his fingers were crossed, not for good luck, but like he was covering a lie.

***

"That's a bit theatrical." Hunter laughs at me. I am surprised he doesn't have a cigarette in his hand.

We are sitting on the bathroom floor, facing each other, but I look away from him.

"Not the pain," he clarifies, "I mean Christ's disappointment."

I don't speak.

"That's a bit of a projection, don't you think?"

I look back at him, shrugging.

He laughs and shakes his head. "Can I see it again?"

I lower the towel as I tuck my feet under me and shift my weight onto one hip.

He furrows his eyebrows.

"What?"

"I was hoping I could see your heartbeat."

"Oh, yeah," I say, "I don't have a heart anymore."

He laughs through his nose and sits back away from me. I cover myself, pulling the towel tighter.

"So," Hunter drags out the vowel, "are you still married?"

"Well ... technically ... on paper—"

"It's a yes or no question." There is an edge to his voice.

He must be tired. He must regret listening to me. If he lets me continue, it will not get easier, so I don't say anything but I do cross my fingers.

"I'm sorry," he says, grabbing a cigarette and spinning it between his fingers. "I don't know why that sounded so mean."

"It's okay."

"No, it's not." He lights the cigarette and gestures for me to continue. "Please, you were telling me about how you became heartless. Proceed."

TRACK 9: "WASTED AND READY"

I heard once that the right thing to do and the hard thing to do are usually the same—like family dinners during the holidays. You know there will be arguments. You'll get angry and embarrass yourself in front of your grandmother, your father will get drunk, your mother will be embarrassed, and everyone will ride home in silence with the windows down, as if the vortex inside the car can carry away the carbon monoxide, cigarette ashes, and hard feelings. But every year you go to dinner, and you do it all again.

It felt like I was doing the right thing. I expected the right thing to be hard. It's so confusing, you know? What if the wrong thing is just as hard as the right thing? How do you know?

When I came back to Kentucky, I scrambled to fill my time with last-minute weddings. I slashed my prices like a Mattress King was getting a divorce. I gave away free sessions just to get future bookings. Couples were gobbling me up like a Black Friday impulse buy. I was booking the rest of the year solid with a fraction of the income. The problem was, my marriage wasn't the kind that shared bank accounts. He had his credit score, and I had mine. He had his independence, and I had mine.

To make up for the lost income, I started second shooting for other photographers. I gave my weekends to happy couples who never learned my name. I took money from photographers who made it very clear they didn't even need me. They just liked extra income from adding on a second shooter to a wedding package. If anything, it was a huge headache to sift through my files on top of their own—their words, not mine.

I was hired for theater. I gave couples the appearance of double the photos, double the pleasure and double the wealth of memories. If something went terribly wrong with the *real* photographer's gear, or they died in a car accident on the way home, my photos were also for back up.

It was nice to be paid to be superficial. I just lifted up my camera every now and then, only when the moment was really good. Then I stood on the sidelines, invisible. A ghost with a paycheck.

One wedding in July was in one of those old hotels turned "premier establishment to make any event unforgettable." In other words, its historic bones were bastardized by Pinterest influencers. This wedding was money themed. Rich white people danced in a stained-glass ballroom as top tier bourbon sloshed out of their crystal glasses onto their Italian leather shoes. The wait staff was primarily Black people lined along the wall, every ten feet or so, poised to serve the wealthy. The entire guest list stayed inside the central orb of elaborate floral centerpieces while those not invited to the party orbited around the perimeter, darting in only to clean a dish, or deliver more amber liquid.

Towards the end of the night, I wandered around the ballroom, watching the wait staff. Colorful DJ lights flashed on their smiling faces. I wanted to be outraged. I wanted to point my fingers and stomp my feet. *Does no one see this anachronistic bullshit? Is it even anachronistic?* But everyone smiled—staff and guests alike. The air vibrated with pop melodies and rap beats, white cotton and black silk ties, and ice water and liquid courage. I watched as the staff snuck closer to one another, whispered in one another's ears, and laughed. I photographed them instead.

They soaked it up. They slung their arms over one another and smiled at my camera. They lifted their hands, shifted their hips back and forth together, and sang. Their joy was contagious.

"Excuse me," a guest interjected. She grabbed my elbow like she had paid for me to be there. "What are you doing?"

She smelt of wine that had gone bad, soured in a hot window sill. She shook me. "The father of the bride is with his daughter and no one is photographing it." She pointed with the hand that held her wine glass and I saw the father. His tie was loosened, his coat was askew, and he held a drink in each hand. It would not be a photo for the mantle.

Wiggling out of her grip, I told the woman, "I promise, I have tons of photos of the bride and father together." It wouldn't do any good to tell her none of my photos would end up in the wedding album, I wasn't the *real* photographer.

"You're telling me no?" Her body whipped back away from me like I had assaulted her.

The primary photographer caught my attention from the cake table. A slice of cake on a plate in his hand. His head tilted up and to the side, as if to ask me, *what's going on?*

"No," I told the woman, "I mean, I'd be happy to photograph this moment as well." Then I walked away, my hands shaking. My elbow ached from the pressure of her grip as I photographed the father and his daughter. Both of them turned away from my camera as if uninterested in capturing the moment.

My hands shook until I left the ballroom, rode the elevator to the street, and lit a cigarette. Even then, pacing was the only way to hide the trembling. I wanted to leave but had an hour left on my contract. Even if I had the courage to leave early, I didn't want to go home.

Two wedding guests emerged from the building—a man and woman. They were walking fast and whispering angrily. He had done something.

"Don't bother coming home," she said, loudly enough for me to hear. He stopped walking, plunged his hands into his pockets, and spun back towards the door. When his gaze caught mine, he pulled a cigarette pack from his inside coat pocket and shook it like he hoped one last cigarette would fall out, but it was empty.

I offered him a cigarette and his eyes scanned me from my head to my toe. It's just like a man to do whatever he wants with his eyes.

"Are you a man or a woman?"

I was in the standard vendor uniform: black slacks and a white button-up shirt. Ironically, my husband had made a similar comment but with the added suggestion of padding a bra so I looked more feminine. I had slipped my bra off through my shirt sleeve and thrown it at him.

This man said it differently, though. He looked at me differently, like the mystery was part of the appeal.

I hunted his face and limbs for signs of intoxication. He didn't slur and he didn't sway. He just stared back at me, took a draw of his cigarette, and inched closer to me. We were in some sort of staring contest or game of chicken. He was looking at me like he was daring me to turn him away. The truth was, I liked being seen. I liked knowing what kind of girlfriend or wife he had—the curvy female type that my dad would have whistled at—and then knowing that he was looking at me like I was in the same category.

I led him to a small empty ballroom where they stored stacks of chairs, where I had hidden to eat my vendor's meal earlier that night— reheated spaghetti and dry toast—with plastic cutlery. I thought about spaghetti the entire time the man covered me in wet kisses and then his cum.

***

Hunter hasn't blinked in a while.

He is slouched on the floor with his back to the sink cabinet and his arms crossed over his chest. He is only in a towel and his hair is still damp. I wonder if I need to finish the story or if he gets the gist.

It feels good, actually. I didn't expect to be empowered by releasing this secret I've been holding on to. I am silently crying but no longer tears of pain or shame. I do not think it will earn me pity either way. I am crying because I feel physically lighter, like my chest can fully expand, at last.

Hunter doesn't speak, his eyes are focused on some distant point.

"I did this sort of thing for a while." I say, "Somewhere along the way, I got good at finding men who looked at me a certain way. Like, members of a fight club, only, a *fuck* club. Mostly married men who liked that 'ambiguous gender thing.' I was their gateway-sexual-orientation experiment. I felt exotic with them." I stop speaking when I realize I am rubbing the spot where my wedding band once was.

Hunter notices.

"I could spin my wedding band, take it off and put it back on. If they did the same, we passed each other's silent code of ethics; neither of us would risk getting caught and neither of us wanted a relationship or a savior—just the forbidden fruit, the knowledge of the difference between good and evil."

Hunter winces. It is the first obvious sign that he is uncomfortable. I would normally stop for his sake but for some reason, I don't.

"Sometimes I was wrong. I would think a man had looked at me in that way that I recognized but then he would recoil, like he would never dream of acting on whatever fantasies played out behind his irises. When this happened, I'd go home and lay in bed, scrolling the casual encounters section of craigslist."

"Jesus Christ."

"I know what you're thinking. How dangerous or dumb. I could have gotten raped or murdered, but let's be real. I can get raped and murdered going to the grocery store. If I don't get raped and murdered, I get a lot more out of a casual encounter than I do at the grocery store. More bang for my buck, you know?"

It's a bad joke and neither of us laugh. The neglected cherry of

Hunter's cigarette falls on top of his knee. He exclaims as it burns his skin until he knocks it off.

"You doin' okay over there?" I ask.

"Yeah, I mean, I don't know at this point," Hunter says, relighting his cigarette. "I think I know where this is going. I'm just confused. Why are you telling me this?"

I am sitting with my back to the wall across from him, we are both only in a towel. We are just far enough that our legs don't touch, but if I reach out and extend my arm as far as it will go, I can reach the pink-skinned burn on his knee. My thumb traces around the edges of the small spot for no other reason than to allow the urge to fix it to build up inside of me. To let the desire to ease his pain with a medically useless kiss of my lips, fester into something that I think is love.

I draw my hand back. "Why aren't you asking me questions? Why are you just letting me talk?"

He shrugs. Then, as if he's changed his mind, he says, "Okay, why not just leave your husband? Why …" He waves his hands. "… do all this?"

"I don't know," I say. "Because it felt like it was working for a while. Because I was numb to our brand of normal. Because the longer I stayed in the dark, the harsher the sun felt when I saw it. And, because he didn't leave me either. He could have left. We didn't have kids or loans. We rented. He had a good job. When I would talk about leaving or about being unhappy, he'd beg me to stay. He'd promise things would be better. A part of me thought he knew what I was doing but wouldn't say it aloud, like he was ashamed of it but somehow understood. So, I didn't mention it either."

Hunter exhales as he lets his head fall against the cabinet behind him. "I don't get that."

We are silent. I listen for the crackle of his cigarette but it has burned out again.

"So, you just slept with lots of strangers?"

"I mean …" I refrain from rolling my eyes. "What's a lot?"

He laughs, struggling for words. "I guess I don't know."

"How many women have you been with?" I ask, boldly.

He looks at the ceiling as if it will help him count. His pointer finger is bouncing between his other nine fingers and I realize he has made it back to his left hand for round two. He is already in the double digits. He says, "I don't know like, fifteen maybe."

I lean forward. "Fifteen? Fuck," I say, "I went through a mid-life crisis and barely made it to fifteen, you included." I jerk my chin towards him and then throw myself back towards the wall and cross my arms over my chest. I am actually furious. I have held the same double digits like a scarlet letter. I think of how I cried when I slept with the tenth man—a casual encounter. A man named Dominic, who's ad included a Dominos vegetable pizza, who told me I was too pretty to be on craigslist, and who treated me like I was on a date and not just a casual encounter. There's a difference, you know? I had cried all the way home, when I left early the next morning because I knew I wouldn't feel again until someone else touched me like he had.

Hunter's shoulders are high, close to his ears. "But that's fifteen since I lost my virginity, with people I *knew*. There are diseases that come from this kind of recklessness."

I am crying again, aware of the damp coldness of my hair and the towel and the fear that nothing will be warm again. "I told you it was bad news."

TRACK 10: "HEART IT RACES"

It was Halloween, and for all intents and purposes, I was naked, legs like spiders in cold metal stirrups. The doctor was dressed like a dalmatian. Her floppy, black ears bounced as she shoved utensils into my cervix and asked me about my sexual activity.

"What was your husband treated for?"

"Chlamydia." I swallowed the urge to quit the word halfway through.

"It could be worse." The assistant nurse patted my shoulder. Thankfully, she was dressed like a nurse.

"And your husband notified you of his infection today?"

I nodded, all too aware that they had assumed he had given it to me—that I was the innocent one.

In response to the question, all I could do was nod. Tears carved a salty path to the corner of my downturned lips. I tasted the Pacific Ocean.

The nurse offered me a tissue. "It's going to be alright. Chlamydia is basically just a cold. If you test positive, you'll be over it before we even get the results back."

"Do you feel any pain?" The doctor stood, pushing down on my abdomen.

I felt conflicted when I answered the question with a no, wondering what kind of pain she might be referring to. The doctor moved to my side. She lifted up the paper gown they'd given me to feel modest and proceeded with a breast exam.

Her dalmatian ears dangled back and forth with the motion of her peeking at the tattoo on my rib cage. "I bet that hurt."

I cried then, in a self-exorcism kind of way. They both stroked my hair and covered me in my coat. When the body shakes and tears finally subsided, she instructed me that I could get dressed, but I could take my time.

When the doctor and the nurse left, I shed the paper gown and stood naked in the middle of the room—skin yellow from the fluorescent lights, chilled by the air coming from the vents—and I thought about how slow I was to acknowledge the severity of my situation, how fast water rose, and how numb my skin grew. I distracted myself with anxieties and worst-case scenarios, but I didn't notice the slow creep of the shadows as they grew longer and longer, until everything was shrouded in their darkness, filtered in black and stripped of detail.

When I looked around everything was underexposed, like a bad photo that couldn't be saved by even the best image editing software. Whatever I hoped to capture was lost and all that remained were the grainy ghosts of what I had hoped to have instead. The settings on the camera were wrong, or maybe I just wasn't ready. The darkness was all that was captured and all that remained.

I put on my clothes and cracked the door to notify the doctor I was ready.

After she came back, hesitant and kind, I listened to her explain how I would go ahead and take the antibiotic to treat the STI. They wouldn't get the results of the test for a couple of weeks, which meant, in a couple weeks-time, I would find out that either I never had chlamydia or I no longer had it—a painfully appropriate metaphor for my marriage.

My mother was parked outside the Health Department because I had been too distraught to drive myself. She was quiet as she drove me to her house for a late lunch.

I tried to eat the BLT she offered me but couldn't stop thinking about how my inner thighs felt sticky and I was spreading Chlamydia all over my parent's dining room while they argued about who had tracked mud through the house.

My mother called my father a five-year-old child. My father called my mother a nag. They proceeded to mumble angrily to themselves while I stared at the uneaten food on my plate, looking for a saint's face in the toast.

"You'll work it out," my mom said, patting my shoulder.

"Boys will be boys," my father volunteered from his sunken spot on the couch, holding his tea spiked with whiskey in one hand and a Marlboro light in the other.

My mother shook her head, rolled her eyes, and sat next to me. I had also let them both believe it was him. That he had given me a venereal infection.

"I want to give up," I said, surprising even myself.

My mother didn't look at me as she responded. "Marriage is hard."

"Should it be this hard?" I asked sincerely.

"A successful marriage isn't easy," she recited.

I was frustrated with her parroting motivational quotes from chicken soup for the married soul. I wanted the real answers, the guilty confessions. I wanted to hear she was ready to give up too. I asked her point-blank, "There has to be some point where the suffering is too great and you'll admit quitting is the best viable option."

Her words of rebuttal charged at me but fell on their face, like warriors who had tied their shoes together. Her eyes watered and she seemed to see me differently through the tears, like I was magnified.

It was so quiet I could hear the crinkle of the burning cherry of my father's cigarette. My mother took hold of both my shoulders, and I braced myself for a pep talk—more encouragement for not giving up.

She said, "My grandfather had a cow once. He spent all his money on her. He couldn't even afford a fence. So as a calf, he barely threw a rope around her neck, so that she would stay close to the barn. As the calf grazed, she would only go as far as the rope would let her because she wasn't strong enough to break the rope. Eventually, she got used to staying in one spot whether it was grass or dirt or mud. Even as she grew into a one-ton heifer, she never tested her strength against the rope, because she was so accustomed to thinking she wasn't strong enough."

"Dumb cow," I said.

She laughed. "Sweetie, my grandfather didn't want the cow to know how easily she could escape. He wanted to keep the cow close, and that was just one way to do it. I don't say all this to make you feel dumb. I say this so that you know that you are strong enough to pull that rope clean out of the ground if you want to. I hate that anyone has made you think otherwise."

I said, "I can't believe you're calling me a heifer."

"Sweetie," she said, tilting her head at me, "Do you know what I mean?"

I thought I did.

***

"Do you remember a night, maybe a month ago—where you logged into my account on that music streaming app?" Hunter asks, more relaxed now.

"You knew I was listening?"

"I didn't," he says. "I mean, I hoped it was you."

I nod. "I wasn't sure either."

"What were you doing then?"

I understand now he is still thinking about me with other people. "Letting go," I say with a hopeful smile. "Breaking free. Having a heart-of-the-ocean moment."

TRACK 11: "I WANT YOU"

It smelled like fair season, like funnel cakes and Ferris wheel engine exhaust. The scent of mums and pumpkins lingered in the evening as Jodie and I zig zagged aimlessly across county lines.

A local band played over the radio via your music app, which paused and sputtered as we lost service.

"What's the threshold for a marriage to break?" I asked out of the blue. "Like, you can tell it's bulging and splintering but it hasn't sunk yet."

"Marriage is a boat?" Jodie asked.

"A big boat, like the Titanic. Like, you've already hit the iceberg, that sneaky bitch in the night, and now you're just waiting for the thing to sink. At what point do you jump? Or do you ride it all the way until the end?"

Jodie smoked her cigarette and stared out over the dashboard. She said, "So, in this analogy, are you waiting for a safety boat to open up? Or are you waiting around because you think you can die with your third-class lover?"

"I have no lover at all," I said, "just an unwanted marriage and a great big ocean to die in."

Jodie nearly choked on her cigarette. "Damn, babe. Can we pretend you haven't jumped off the back of the boat yet? I ask because Rose nearly kills herself thinking she could have it all if she just waits a little while longer. She thinks she can survive without a lifeboat."

I think for a minute and then ask, "You think she should have stayed on the first lifeboat when she had the chance?"

"No," Jodie said. "I think she would have regretted that," and after a pause, added, "but my point is, she barely survived."

"So, I should get on the lifeboat, be quiet, and be glad I'm not dead?"

"I don't like this analogy. For the sake of a glass half full approach, let's say you're not on the Titanic yet. You're just with an asshole that is about to get on the Titanic. You could stay with him, be miserable until you meet some poor artist who draws you naked or some shit. You learn the hard way that you'd rather die than stay with the asshole. OR!" She slapped me on the shoulder. "You listen to your gut. You don't get on the Titanic. You stay on land, alone … maybe get a cat."

I navigated around a pothole while Tommy and the High Pilots played. I visualized the new metaphor with varying degrees of tragedy.

"My question is," Jodie continued, "you seem to have checked out months ago. Not only did you annoy the shit out of me talking about your San Fran man, you've slept with other people! You're an adulterer now. What are you clinging to? Why don't you leave?"

"I'm tired of that question," I said as my hand migrated to my bangs, combing them back. "Did I really talk about Hunter that much?"

"Once, you called me at two in the morning. You were so drunk, all you said was," in an offensively inaccurate whiny tone she imitated me, "do you think he eats fish sticks? Do you think he thinks about me when he eats fish sticks?"

"What did you tell me?" I asked with a smirk.

"You didn't let me answer!" She laughed. "You just hung up and ignored my call back."

The music stopped. Another song began.

"What just happened?" Jodie asked, staring at the radio as if it might answer.

I picked up my phone and looked: a name I didn't recognize, another local band maybe.

"I think it's Hunter," I said.

"What do you mean it's Hunter?"

"It's his account I use. I think sometimes he gets on there while I'm playing music and plays other music."

As I crossed a concrete bridge over the creek, I navigated the car up a steep hill over a cattle guard. Jodie stared and smiled at me.

"So, let me get this straight." She put her elbow out the window and turned toward me. "You just drive around and listen to the music Hunter is listening to?"

"I'm not sure how it works. I think he, like, DJs my playlist," I said. "I can't listen when he's using it. I can only change the songs."

"Story." Jodie emphasized the period. "Your Titanic is sinking to the playlist of a man who had you on a mattress in the back of an Astro van in a roadside rest area."

A new tragedy emerged: the image of me in an ice-field clinging to my cell phone quietly dying from the cold water rushing into its electronics, interrupting the soundtrack to my soul's impending doom.

My car reached the top of the hill where the road meandered through a thin patch of trees and popped us out onto an overpass over

Interstate 64.

I stopped the car in the middle of the bridge over the eastbound lanes.

Jodie asked me, "Why don't you just contact him?"

"Hunter?" I asked, as if there was anyone else. "We didn't exchange numbers."

Jodie reminded me, "We live in a modern society. You know how to stalk someone."

I actually hadn't stalked you. I hadn't dared tempt myself. "He's too good for me," I told her.

Jodie rolled her eyes. She picked up my phone, stopped the music, and played Usher's "You got it bad".

"Sorry, Hunter, this is why you don't log into strangers' phones."

Panicked, I scrambled for my phone, but my seat belt held me at bay. Jodie extended her arm out her window in a game of keep-away.

Then, you selected another song. It was filled with bass lines and what I can only describe as jazzy beat boxing. Jodie looked at my phone, the song was titled "Thinkin' about your body."

A wicked smile spread across Jodie's face. The roar of a semi passing under the bridge shook my car but I could still hear Jodie say, what were were both thinking. "He is talking to you through songs right now."

I didn't want to say it was so. I didn't want to break the spell. Sometimes, I changed songs on you, and you left the app entirely. Maybe, you thought your phone was possessed. Or maybe, you were lying with another person in the back of your Astro van. Maybe some other soul was clinging to you in an ice-feild.

Jodie played another song: Blink 182's "I miss you."

We waited. The song barely made it through the first verse when it changed to Nick Lowe's "I trained her to love me."

I told Jodie to play "Come back from San Francisco" by the

Magnetic Fields.

You selected Tom Waits' "Long way home."

"Play Tom Petty!" I yelled. "The Waiting!"

I cranked the volume and bolted from the driver's seat. Immersed in the night, Tom Petty sang my thoughts for me as I waited for the next message from you to come in. My car door went *ding, ding, ding,* warning me, but I didn't listen.

A harmonica took over the speakers in my car. A nasally voice sang fast and characteristically Bob Dylan.

I wanted to believe it was you, telling me, *I want you.* Then, my phone rang. I swear to God, I thought it was, impossibly, you.

Jodie's tone told me it was not you. She rejected the phone call and got out of the car. Dylan returned for a moment before my phone rang again. Jodie flashed the caller ID my way, and I shook my head. I registered that Jodie answered it for me, but I had zoned out. I was over-stimulated and emotionally exhausted. I bent over and tried to catch my breath between reflectors on the double lines in the middle of the road, in the middle of the night, in the middle of going nowhere.

When I felt Jodie's hand on my shoulder, the song of the crickets rushed back to my ears, punctuated by my car doors' warning bell. *Ding, ding, ding.*

"I have some, well, I don't know if it's good or bad news. I don't know what's good or bad anymore." Jodie sighed. "I have news."

"Hit me with it," I said.

"It turns out that your test came back negative."

"What test?" I asked.

"Your pap smear results came in the mail. Your husband found them and I guess put two and two together. You're STI free by the way. And if you can't do the math, this means he picked up an STI all on his own."

I stood up straight.

"He says he's very sorry," Jodie said with an almost audible eye roll.

"But I'm clean?" I asked her.

Jodie nodded and flashed a hesitant smile.

I leaned back to face the night sky as if looking for answers between the stars and their blinking morse code messages. Thinking maybe a jet would connect some dots.

I put my hands on my hips and looked at Jodie. "Are you thinking what I'm thinking?"

"Probably not," she said. "Does it involve lighting something on fire?"

"You remember when Rose climbs on the railing?" I asked.

Her face recomposed into something strange and fierce. "Yes, of course."

She followed me toward the railing of the bridge. Headlights from the eastbound lanes missed us, leaving us in the dark as we stepped up.

My rings slipped off my left hand with ease.

"Oh, thank God," Jodie said, clutching her chest. "A part of me was afraid this was a *you jump, I jump* situation."

Mid laugh, without a countdown, or a salutation, or even a second thought, the diamond ring and the gold band fell from my fingers and landed on the asphalt below with a puny, imperceptible *tink* lost to the roar of tires on asphalt and crickets, and my car door begging me to get back into the car and move on. *Ding, ding, ding.*

***

"So, you're divorced?" Hunter grabs my foot, pulls it to his lap, and rubs the arch with his thumb.

"Technically," I repeat the word sarcastically, "no, but it's all filed. I'm just waiting for the paperwork."

The pressure of his thumb is light. His pants are balled up next to him and he digs in the pockets with his other hand. He pulls out a bright pink penis-shaped wine glass charm. "This wasn't a New Year's Eve party, was it?"

I shake my head.

"Is your ex-husband in the freezer?"

I laugh and swat his legs. "Do I look like someone who could cut up a body?"

"I truly don't know. You have this thing about you, like you are a pandora's box, like it would be unwise to open you up in a public place."

We both laugh.

"It's a cake," I confess. "In the freezer. It's the two year old top of our wedding cake. We forgot to eat it after the first year."

"That's probably why you two didn't make it," Hunter says with a smirk.

"I'll never not eat a year old cake again," I say.

"I meant that as a compliment, by the way." Hunter says, taking our conversation back a few steps. "I like that you are more than you appear. Like you have secrets worth digging up."

TRACK 12: "BRILLIANT DISGUISE"

You kept your secrets too, you know.

You didn't tell me you played music. You didn't warn me that someday, I'd go into a bar in Kentucky, stand in the front row, and watch you sing and play guitar.

Jodie insisted I go out, claimed that, besides getting married, divorce was the best and most efficient way to get free drinks, and no one had to put out if they don't want to.

When we arrived, Jodie walked right up to two young men at the bar. She was prepared to play the divorce card if she had to. She said, "Hey, we have a divorce party to plan. Is there any chance you would be kind enough to offer up your seats for the cause?"

The two men looked between Jodie and me and then looked us both up and down. "Divorce from each other?"

Jodie didn't miss a beat. "Ain't that the saddest shit you ever heard? Makes you want to buy us a drink too, doesn't it?"

They did buy us drinks. When the band started playing, the bar cleared out and headed to the room with the stage. We had the bar to ourselves and could still hear the show. By the middle of the first band's set, we were picking out what to catch on fire for the divorce celebration.

I told her, "I still have the top of my wedding cake. We completely forgot about it for our first anniversary."

"That's disgusting," she said. "Everybody's just trying to have their cake and eat it too, and they're willing to settle for stale, year old, freezer burnt cake."

We were deciding to have the party on New Year's Eve, when the first band left the stage and Jodie got distracted. She was watching the doors and the archways that led to the room with the stage. I suggested we risk our seats and go smoke, but she claimed she was too cold.

When the next band started playing, she snatched my hand and drug me into a crowded side room with a stage at the end. The drummer and bassist sound checked while Jodie elbowed our way to the front row.

Then you appeared. You were shaggier and thicker than the last time I had seen you. I tried to recoil back into the crowd, but Jodie wouldn't let me. There would have been no use. The crowd behind me was packed too tightly. I was stuck. Frankie followed you on stage. He looked naked, holding only a magazine over himself.

Frankie sat down off to the side, crossed his legs, and read a poem. At the end, when Frankie said "Will you marry it, marry it, marry it", you raised your fist in the air. As it came down on the last word, the band started, all in time, all loud and rock and roll. It was impressive. You are really talented. You know the way your band seemed to be on their toes? That's how I felt too. I felt present and invincible. Invisible and alive. I was lost in the crowd, floating in the room with guitar riffs bouncing around me, swelling up and down, until our eyes met.

I felt like a deer in headlights, and I don't mean that in the cliche way. I mean, your eyes hit me like an eighty-mile-per-hour set of headlights. My body felt the surge of endorphins, as if it was preparing for the end, hoping a last boost of chemicals would dull the pain of a truck driving right through my heart. My last hope was that maybe you wouldn't recognize me in my orangish blonde hair.

But you did.

You stepped down from the stage and slipped your guitar up and over me, playing it behind my back. You smelled just like I remembered.

You whispered in my ear, but I couldn't hear the words. What was it you said?

***

Hunter is standing up now, his hand extended towards me to help me to my feet. "I asked you: Is that you? Or just a brilliant disguise?"

I take his hand, rise to my feet, and ask him, "What kind of guitar was that, that you were playing?"

"It's called a Reverend," Hunter says. The glint in his eyes tells me he is thinking about my body and not the fact that a Reverend bound us together that night.

He pulls me close. My towel loosens as he wraps his arms around me. "I do have a confession," he says. "Jodie set it up, despite my refusal. I told Jodie not to come to the bar, not to bring you."

My eyes flash open, I don't know if he pushes me away or I pull myself away. "Yeah, that makes sense," I say.

Hunter searches my eyes. "She must have tracked me down through my radio show. She emailed me and said that she thought I should know you never forgot me. I told her you were more of a dream to me than a real person. I wasn't sure I could separate the two."

The words are dense, closed off to me like those Russian dolls I can't pronounce the name of. I keep thinking I have cracked them open, only to find another deeper meaning.

He whispers again, "But I think I'd rather get lost between the two than not know what would happen if I never tried."

And, just like that, I forget about the fucking dolls and free-fall into place. Hunter turns and walks away from me. At my side I see my reflection in the mirror over the sink. My orange hair has air dried in soft, full waves. My towel is a deep forest green, and I'm reminded of a painting of Persephone by a pre-Raphaelite I don't remember the name of. I resemble the goddess of the underworld.

Hunter whistles at me as he admires me from the doorway. What if he is my mythical hero who has traveled through hell to rescue me from the underworld. Maybe he is not my savior, but Hades, my captor, my king of the underworld.

"As much as I enjoy you naked, I'd suggest a coat." Hunter's words bring me back to the bathroom where, if I am a goddess of anything, it is this bathroom: its dirty walls, thirty year old linoleum floor, full ashtray, and tray of sea shells.

"Are we going outside?" I ask.

He slaps the doorjamb and smiles at me. "Let's blow up some cake." When he disappears from the doorway, I can see the sky through the kitchen brighten with the sunrise. Cool blue light filters into the apartment, dispelling the darkness inside and out.

Tuesday Night Playlist

TRACK 13: "AT THE BOTTOM OF EVERYTHING"

Christmas Eve, 2013

I am going the wrong direction.

I am somewhere between yesterday and today, somewhere between age twenty-six and twenty-seven, somewhere between asleep and wide awake, on a plane somewhere between home and Rome, somewhere between a window over a dark ocean and a woman with a serene look on her face. I hope this works. If not, I'll have let down my mother and lied to Hunter for nothing.

The plane begins to violently shake.

Lights come on in the cabin, but no one says anything, not the pilot, a flight attendant, or any passenger within earshot. I keep waiting for someone to say something, anything. *It's alright folks*, or

Please return to your seats and fasten your seatbelts, or *Prepare the cabin for emergency landing.*

I look out the window at a morning sky between dawn and day, and then I look at the woman next to me, now awake. Her eyes are sleepy but her face is stern. She offers me the smallest, weakest smile.

As the plane vibrates, I think about the label on an aerosol can that reads: *DO NOT SHAKE.*

I shook an aerosol can once. The air came out frosty, like the sheen of ice on Rose and Jack as they waited to die.

A light on the wing blinks through the layer of condensation on my window. It is foggy and distant like a life-boat too far to hear my cries for help. I can make out frost forming on the wings. As the turbulence grows, I wonder how many engines are still working. *Why have the pilots not said anything?*

They probably know we only have a short time left to live: ninety seconds tops. They are spending their last minute and a half praying to a god or kissing a photo of their family. I can't hold that against them. The passengers waste the first half of their last ninety seconds convincing themselves the plane will sort itself out.

Thirty seconds to go and no one in the cabin can continue to ignore the downward, too-sharp angle of the vessel. Collectively, their guts scream. We don't get the rest of our thirty seconds to live, because the world isn't fair. The speed of our spiral into the Atlantic Ocean causes the plane to break in half. We all die instantly.

The best news is the violent shaking stops. It is a peace I have never known before. A freefall through a cosmic space without friction or weight, until I begin to shake again.

"Sir!"

Hands are on my shoulders, shaking me gently.

"Sir? Ma'am?" A female voice speaks. I don't recognize it. "Where's the water? Ma'am, come back to us."

Little by little, the color seeps into my vision as I register my surroundings.

I am on the floor.

I am in a doorway.

My pants are around my knees. I remember going to the bathroom. My hands are sunken into the sweaty fibers of my shirt. My thighs are crammed into the too-small space of the lavatory. I am pulled across the floor and stretched out.

Someone pulls my jeans up and over my thighs, says I am a she.

Someone puts two fingers on my wrist and finds my pulse, says I have a boy's haircut.

Someone fans me with a Skymall magazine, as they lament, they don't know what to call anyone these days.

"What happened?" I hear someone ask from over top of me.

"I think he—I mean, she—passed out."

"Do you think they're on something?"

My eyelid is held open, and a small flashlight flashes across my eyes.

"No, I think they just fainted. Could be dehydrated."

A glass of water tilts towards my mouth.

"Can we get her back to her seat?"

Arms wiggle beneath my shoulders, and I am propped up. Someone keeps calling me honey. "Come on, honey. You've only fainted. You're okay, honey. Everything's okay."

I am able to focus my eyes on her. She is the woman assigned to the aisle seat in my row. Her back is to the light of the plane's lavatory. She still holds a glowing cup of water out to me. I try to sit up, letting someone behind me help. When my hand finally clasps the cup of water, I chug it.

"I'm sorry," I say, gasping for air.

"For what?"

She offers me a pack of peanuts, and even though I hate peanuts, I stuff them in my mouth between words. "For … passing out. Causing … a scene."

"Just glad you're okay sweetheart." The woman at my back moves to the side of me—a flight attendant. She says, "Do you think we need to contact a doctor?"

"No," I say too quickly. "I'm fine. I'm sorry about all this."

"Okay. Let's get you back to your seat."

"I'm really sorry," I say, accepting their help to get to my seat.

"And what exactly are you apologizing for?"

"I just didn't mean to scare anyone," I say, feeling better with each step. "I passed out this summer too. After my hair caught on fire. The ambulance came and got me, and the doctor told me that I was like one of those girls in the front row of an Elvis show, who passes out with a rush of adrenaline or excitement. And then Elvis told me I was the devil. So, I think it was just the turbulence of the plane that scared me." Then, because I think it is relevant, I add, "Plus, it's my birthday."

"I see," she says as she guides me back into my seat and retrieves my coat from the floor. I drape it over my legs and find another bag of peanuts in my hand.

"Tell you what," she says, settling into the seat next to me. "My name is Janet, by the way. How about we talk for a while. Tell me about yourself. What's your name?"

I laugh to myself as I stuff peanuts in my mouth. "My name is Story," I say. "Story like the word. No special spelling. Nothing fancy. Just plain old s-t-o-r-y."

The flight attendant hands Janet two steaming cups and she passes one to me. It is tea. The warmth spreads across my tongue, down my throat, and into my belly.

"First off, happy birthday, Story," Janet says, tapping the side of her tea. "And second, let's see, you said you have been fainting a lot? And there was that bit about the devil and Elvis? I do wonder why you are going to Rome. Where to begin?"

TRACK 14: "RUNNIN' ON EMPTY"

I suspect it began with my father dying. It happened like a rug had been ripped out from under me. That rug had been thrown over a pit, like a trap, I've not been able to claw my way out.

The last time I saw him alive was Easter. We had planned to eat an early dinner, but Dad wasn't hungry. He promised we could eat after he watched The Weather Channel. He was always watching the weather. You could say storms came easy to him.

As my mom paced the kitchen with rosary beads in her hands, I whispered to my father, "What'd ya do?"

He shook his head. "Hell if I know. If she tells you, let me know."

Mom stopped her pacing. Her gaze was fierce on my father and then softer on me. "A new pope was elected today," she said. "I think he's a good one."

My father looked at me. "She thinks the pope can do no wrong."

"He's the pope," my mom called over her shoulder.

"He's gotta change the oil and wipe shit from his ass just like the rest of us," my father said in a low voice to me, like he thought I was a stand-in for one of his drinking buddies.

Mom glared at him. I could see the threat in her eyes, like she would bring the pope to our house and he would fix him somehow. My father was immune to such threats. Mom was alone in her faith.

"The pope doesn't change the oil," my mom added with a smirk. "He has a chauffeur."

My dad laughed, and the spirits were raised for a moment. Then, he looked at me and asked, "When's the last time you checked the oil in your car?"

I couldn't remember a time that I was willing to admit to, so I just shrugged.

He shook his head at me, happy to have a bigger disappointment in the room. He said, "I've told you time and time again, you need to check the oil. Cars can't run without oil."

"I know. I haven't had time to take it to the shop," I said with my eyes on his cup of tea, the stench of whiskey strong enough to smell from across the living room.

He groaned as he stood up from the couch, sucked hard on a cigarette, and smashed it into a clay ashtray I'd made in middle school. He said, "I think I've got some extra oil in the truck. I'm gonna teach you how to change it."

"Don't you dirty those clothes," my mom said with her hands on her hips. "I'm tired of cleaning engine oil off of your good jeans."

"Alright, alright," he said, straightening his back, face grimacing with the pain. He patted me on the shoulder and told me he'd change and meet me outside.

The afternoon was hot, even under the canopy of the trees around the house. Hail-damaged sheet metal bounced dappled sunlight into my eyes. The gravel crunched as I dodged daffodils around my father's prized possession: a bright blue 1990 Corvette ZR-1. It was on blocks and covered with a tarp like a caged animal. The "Corvette from Hell" my dad had named it, because all the go-parts worked but none of the stopping-parts worked. He'd say it like it was a badge of honor to be unstoppable.

The screen door slammed. My dad walked with a crook in his spine as he dodged the same daffodils. He sat his mug on the bumper and rummaged through the toolbox in his truck bed. I popped the hood of my car and waited for instructions.

My dad pulled out a large oil-stained jug, walked it over to my car, twisted off the cap, and smelled it. "Yep, that's oil. You never know what I might put in a container. Always best to check," he said, grinning.

"Should we jack her up?" I asked.

"Nah." He waved me off. "Don't know where my jacks are."

"I think I have one," I said. I thought I had it in my trunk, but I had forgotten my trunk release was messed up. I had to press the latch release by the driver side seat and run to catch the latch. I wasn't quite quick enough, though.

"What's wrong with your trunk release?"

I said nothing was wrong.

"Looks like your latch is broke," he said as he stood by the trunk and let me press the release. He inspected the latch and closed the trunk. He asked me to throw my keys to him, so I did. He pushed the keyhole in and twisted it, and the trunk popped open.

"Well," I said.

He used a pair of pocket pliers against the latch mechanism. "Ooops."

I looked over his shoulder and was about to ask when he slammed the trunk shut.

"That's for another day," he said. "We'll just lie on the ground."

We both lay on the gravel. The jagged edges of rock felt like acupuncture against our backs.

My dad wasn't much larger than me. He'd spent most of his life being the guy who was small enough to wedge himself into tight spaces to get to that one part of an engine no one else could get to. Still, my car was low to the ground and our noses scraped the undercarriage as he pointed out the plug in the oil pan that would drain the old oil.

I watched him fight the oil plug to loosen it. When it finally broke loose, a thick black stream of oil shot out into the oil pan between us.

"Damn," he said.

"What's wrong?" I asked.

"It don't look pretty. That's the blackest oil I've seen in a long time," he said. "Black as sin."

The stream of oil was steady and dark as it fell into the pan. The engine cracked and popped above us.

"You know, I'm a lot more comfortable than I thought I'd be," my dad said. "I'm gonna have to come out here and lie in the gravel more often."

"I think you do enough lyin' on the gravel, Dad." I said, thinking of all the times mom had called me to tell me Dad was so drunk he had fallen out of his truck and never even made it inside. He'd deny it, and Mom would point out the pink scars on his palm to prove it. Dad never remembered things quite right.

I was feeling brave with him trapped there beside me, so I asked, "Why do you drink, Dad?"

At first, he didn't say anything. His hands came up to rub his mustache, and then, a single finger pressed against his lip like he was keeping the words quiet. Finally, he said, "I don't know, sweetheart." He paused. " 'cause I'm a dumbass."

I didn't know a single person who thought my dad was a

dumbass. He kept half the cars in the county running.

"I think you can quit, Dad, if you really want to. I think you could do it," I said.

He was silent. He still held that finger to his lips. His jaw moved left and right like he could chew his words up and turn them into something else. His chest deflated, and he closed his eyes. He didn't move.

Whatever was so heavy on his chest, I watched him shake it off and return his gaze to the slow drip of oil into the pan. "I think so too, sometimes, I really do."

He re-screwed the drain plug into the oil pan.

"Alright," he said. "Time to put some fresh oil in the ol' girl." He grunted the whole way as he scooted inch by inch out from under my car. I followed, sharing my own cursing vowels as gravel pierced the thin fabric of my T-shirt and scraped my skin.

When we were both standing, my mind went to whatever had happened at church. I asked him, "How was Easter Mass?"

"Fine," he said, picking up the jug of oil from the ground. When he saw my eyebrows raised, he said, "Christ, it was so dry and stale, I thought I might drown myself in the holy water. But they would have thought I was trying to be baptized, and I just didn't have the energy to be saved again."

My dad started to pour the new oil into the engine. He never would use a funnel. He was always so proud of not needing one. But that day, I watched him struggle with the jug. He cursed as his grip fumbled on the bottle. Oil glistened honey-like down the side of the engine.

"God Dammit!" he cursed as he forced the opening of the jug down into the opening of the filler tube, abandoning the pouring performance all together.

"Damn, I'm tired," he said, like he was logging a complaint with whoever was listening above him. Then he knelt on the gravel and retrieved the oil pan from underneath the car. As he poured the contents into an old five-quart jug, he said, "You remember the Baptist preacher that hangs out outside EZ Stop? He said something to me this morning. What was it?" He looked at me as if I knew.

When he found his words, he snapped into the voice of the preacher at the gas station. " 'Sir, I have a very important question. Sir, do you have Jesus in your heart?' I said, 'Yes, sir. I have Jesus in my heart,' and he said, 'Do you know Christ paid the price for your sins?' I said, 'Yes sir, Christ got the short straw on that deal, Sir.' " My father laughed, not able to help interrupting his own performance.

I shook my head and fought back my own smile.

He continued. " 'Have you been washed in the blood of Jesus Christ?' I said, 'Yes sir, I am cleansed by the blood of Jesus Christ, baptized in the Red River Gorge.' He said, 'Because if you don't truly know that Christ is your Savior, and you are nothing without him, then you can be baptized a sinner and just come out of that river a wet sinner.' "

"Well, if that ain't a perfect name for you." I said it like my mom would have said it, the words scurrying from my mouth like rats.

He slapped me.

He had never slapped me. Never touched me. I remember once, telling him that I remember being spanked. I remember crying at a sliding patio door, looking out at the backyard, being told to pick out my own switch. He had shaken his head at me and denied it. Calmly, he had said, "We never spanked you. We were never allowed to. I wasn't tryin' to go to jail."

My mother had told me I probably just remembered their stories. Apparently, as a child, I had heard my parents describe their punishments and adopted those memories as my own.

But this I felt. This was real. My cheek stung. The impact blinded me for a moment.

"Dammit, Story," he said, as if I'd brought this on. His other hand clenched around the jug of oil he'd drained from my car. He didn't look sorry. He looked angry. He lifted the jug so that I could see it. "I told you to watch the oil. Three quarts drained out of your car. It takes 5 to fill it up. That's not good enough, Story. Not good enough. If you don't check the oil, you're gonna end up on the side of the road, like roadkill. Do you understand me?"

TRACK 15: "I HEAR YOU CALLING"

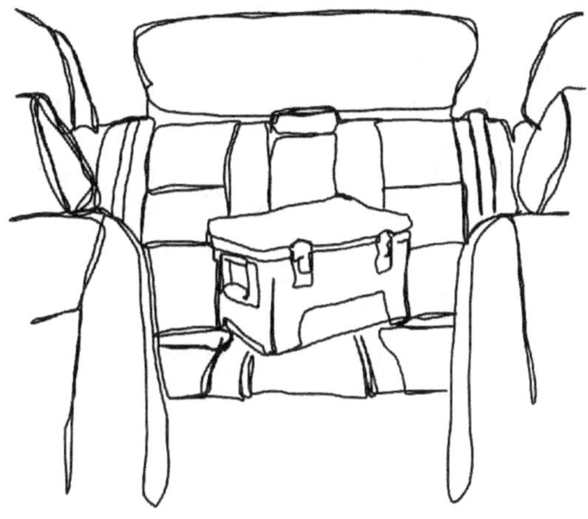

A month later, I photographed a rainy outdoor wedding. Some couples dig that sort of thing; they really embrace it. This was one of those couples. The bride and groom did their first look and bridal portraits in the rain and then said their vows. I didn't dare tell them that my camera wasn't waterproof, that the buttons were messing up, or that if the camera in my hand died, I only had one back up. It would be easily six thousand dollars down the drain for an impromptu Nicholas-Sparks photo shoot.

That's the kind of choices I made for couples. I chalked it up to insurance and didn't blink.

My roommate, Jodie, was with me as an assistant and second photographer. She stood by my side, packing the backup equipment bags and holding an umbrella over me. It was a long day. By the end of it, I felt like a rubber band stretched too tight. As we walked to my car, the grass was slick, and I fell just feet from my car. Jodie just laughed and let me lay there.

Jodie asked for the keys so she could load up the equipment.

"You have the keys," I said.

"Negative," she said, wiggling her fingers at me.

I jammed my fingers into my camera bag, dug around. "I always put them in the backup bag," I told Jodie. "I do that so that I don't leave the backup bag anywhere."

She hunted through the back-up bag, and then her jacket pocket. She apologized, "I don't got 'em, babe."

In my peripheral, I could see her phone flashlight searching through the car windows, into the car. "Uh oh," she said, and I knew what she would say before she said it. "Keys are in the ignition."

I stumbled to my feet, and we both jerked on the car doors like there was a chance the universe would have given us a break.

Jodie asked me if I had AAA.

I said no.

What's worse, our list of people to call was unusually short. We were two hours from home. It was almost midnight. My boyfriend was out of state. My parents were likely in bed. That was the end of my options.

Jodie decided to call her boyfriend, Paul.

I nodded, defeated. Where would we wait while someone came and got us? I would have to confess I'd locked my keys in my car. I had failed the most basic task. How does a professional take thousands of dollars from a client, risk their gear and everything, and then lock their keys in their car? Even if we stayed out in the dark field, probably standing in the rain, I'd still have to come back to the car with a locksmith. Someone would have to let me back onto the grounds. This wasn't a fucking public park; it was a goddamn wedding venue. I'd never get away unnoticed. The shame festered into something that reacted to the cold rain soaked into my bones.

I cursed the skies with my middle fingers to the heavens. "Fuck you!" I yelled at the precipitating darkness.

"Fuck you, rain!" Jodie joined me, even with her phone to her ear.

"Fuck you, gods!" I yelled. "Fuck off. We don't need you anyways!"

We carried on like that, not knocking on wood or anything. Just two petty kids, mad that we'd messed up. Eventually Jodie's boyfriend answered her texts.

While I waited for news of our rescue, my camera bag dug into my shoulder. In a half-crazed disposition, I popped the trunk of my car to load up my equipment into it. I slung it off my shoulder and pushed it off to the side. I closed the trunk. When it slammed, it clicked— realization clicked.

I slung the trunk open again. My dad must have broken my trunk latch—or the lock.

With my knees already perched on the bumper, my head and hands dove into the trunk space, looking for the lever that released the back seats to fold down. When I found it, my fingers were shaking and wet, slipping on the nylon strap. I pulled down and pushed forward with my head. The bench seat in the back moved two or three inches.

The stale moldy air of my interior filtered through to me, and it was like warm sun rays. I leaned into it even more, but only gained a few inches. My mind raced to think of what was in my back seat— what was this new obstacle?

My cooler?

I reached my arm through the opening, contorting my body until my shoulders wedged into the crack. The very tips of my fingers felt for whatever I could push out of the way.

It was the cooler, which was filled with melted ice—water, more fucking water.

I scratched and dug into its plastic lid, desperate to gain any friction to budge it out of the seat.

It worked.

I gained a few more inches in the gap and my head and shoulder squeezed through easily. My other shoulder, chest, and ribs scraped through. My body was doubled over and pressed up against the roof of the interior of my car. I felt like I was emerging from my mother's birth canal, being born all over again.

I was halfway to the keys in the ignition when Jodie knocked on the back seat window, with a phone still to her ear, pointing to the latch on that door. I was trying to get to the keys when I could have just popped the back door open. I reached over and unlocked the godforsaken car.

Jodie flung the door open, still holding her phone to her ear. "Story, you need to call your mom."

***

"Since no one could get a hold of me, my mother had tracked down my boyfriend, who tracked down Jodie's boyfriend, who Jodie just so happened to call for a ride. My mother had told Hunter, my father was in the hospital, and like a cruel game of telephone, he was dead by the time the news got to me."

I brace myself for the apology, the condolences, or the hand touching that leaves me wondering what to say to make someone else feel better.

Janet looks at me and says, "Was it alcohol related?"

Words are lodged at the opening of my mouth like rocks in a cave-in. I shake my head no.

She can't help but show her surprise. It's not her fault though. I'm the one who painted my father out as nothing but a drunk. That has been my problem all along.

TRACK 16: "BLACK CADILLACS"

He died of heart failure, which was surprising because he had a tendency to drive fast and drunk. The roads in eastern Kentucky are dangerous for sober drivers. People back home love to brag that they know their roads with their eyes closed.

It didn't help that my dad knew all the officers and state troopers. He worked on half of their fleet cars and personal cars. I heard once that it's the cops' discretion to arrest or fine a driver for intoxication. If he thinks you're okay, he can let you go. Which also means, if he likes you, he can let you go.

My dad was very charming and likable. He was a professional drunk driver. He was the kind of drunk driver that would stop and help broken down vehicles with a whiskey in his hand. That makes him sound like a good Samaritan, but he made my mom's life hell. She'd hide his keys to keep him from driving drunk, and he'd slash her tires so she couldn't go to work until she gave his keys back.

When he was drunk, he was a different person to her—a mean one. My mom called him Jekyll and Hyde. She'd threaten him with the power of prayer and the pope. Dad would claim he knew God better than anybody. That would make my mother mean. Her words would turn icy and sharp like a winter storm.

I don't mean to paint my mother so poorly. She's the only person I know who never gave up on him. She never left him and never stopped trying to keep him alive. He'd lost a lot of friends in the past few years. Friends, family, and co-workers all slowly faded out of his life. Even I left as soon as I could; I married right out of high school.

Anyways, everyone was surprised that he died so normally, in a bed and not wrapped around a tree, having taken an entire family out with him.

The wake was at my parent's house—my mother's house. Family came in from Eastern Kentucky on my dad's side and Ohio on my mom's side. Both sides drank and smoked cigarettes. The men cried like babies and the women held it together.

Lynyrd Skynyrd albums were passed around as my uncles and aunts told their favorite stories of muscle cars, drag racing, motocross bikes, catfishing, wrestling bears, and doing drugs. They had grown up in the 70s when seat belts, secondhand smoke, and underage drinking didn't hurt anyone. Their hand guns and rifles weren't being used to shoot up elementary schools, yet. Their struggles involved getting laid, getting liquor across county lines, and scraping together pennies for enough gas to race on the straight stretches.

I was left out of the stories. I was either too young or didn't exist yet. They all knew these stories and had recycled them so many times they had probably morphed into new shapes. It was as if they were telling the stories just for me or just for my boyfriend.

My aunt asked me if I knew the story of how my dad was late to marry my mom. She said, "He camped on a boat with my uncles the night before and probably drank too much. They claimed he had fallen asleep in an inflatable donut and drifted off in the night. He woke up floating down the Ohio River, sunburnt as a crab."

My mother shook her head and said, "The lord was trying to save me a world of trouble, but I wouldn't listen."

As everyone laughed, I looked at their wedding photo on the mantle above the ventless fireplace. In an eight by ten inch print, they were posed at the front of a Catholic church, slightly off center. The image had a magenta hue, hiding his sunburn. He looked happy. They both did. He looked like he might float away, or like the giant lapels of his coat would flap and carry him into marital bliss.

My mother told the story about my father's fiftieth birthday, and said, "He'd never been possessed to skydive before. Then, they built that mega-church with that 250-million-dollar statue of Christ. He just couldn't stand it. Every time we'd drive north to see my family, he'd curse and drive like a madman."

"Touchdown Jesus?" Her sister interjected.

"I always called it Butter Jesus," my boyfriend added.

"That's the one." Mom started to laugh. "He hated it. He called it a monstrosity and a waste of money. He said kids were starving in Africa, and this church goes and spends 250 million on an ugly cream colored, papier mâché, legless Messiah."

"Did he think he'd kill himself in protest?" my boyfriend asked.

My mom said, "Worse. He got it in his head that if he went skydiving and didn't die, he'd let the mega church have their mega Jesus."

"Well, we know he survived, so I guess we'll have to visit ol' Butter Jesus the next time we are up that way."

A coy smile crept onto my mother's face. "The statue was struck by lightning and burned down two days later."

The living room erupted in laughter. I sat there thinking about how my father left a smoldering path through his life.

My uncle chimed in to say he'd never met a man so unlucky as my father. He asked my mother, "You remember when he got that Smith and Wesson revolver? He pulled it out of the box, brand new, in his mama's dining room, cocked it, and fired it out the window."

"No one had any idea there would be a live round in it," my mother said, shaking her head. "Can you imagine if that happened today? Somebody would get sued so fast their head would spin. Back then, you just cleaned up the mess and put a new window in."

I sat on the carpet next to the ashtray my dad always used. I listened to story after story of my father jumping train tracks, blowing engines, wrecking cars, and fixing them. Fuck up, fix, fuck up, fix, over and over, until the ashtray overflowed onto the floor. I hadn't realized how much I had drunk. When I watched all these old men drink, I'd drink. Some time late in the night, I guess it all hit me.

I got agitated, and my feet were falling asleep. I didn't want anyone in the house any more. I felt alien, like an outsider in my father's life. Like I missed the best version of him by two decades. Like I'd only gotten to see the sequel, fueled by fermented grain mash and nicotine, leaving me with nothing but a bad taste in my mouth.

My mother told the room she met my dad at a Tom Petty concert. My father had asked for her name, and she refused to give it to him. He followed her, Hans Solo style, and pinned her against a stack of speakers in a field. He'd said he'd do anything for her name and that he'd go to the ends of the earth, for the rest of his days. He'd said they'd write stories about his love for her.

"That's where the name Story came from," my mom pointed at me.

The details are a little hazy, but I believe I told my mother to shut up. I remember a piercing silence. Then, my mom whispered to me to go lie down in her bed. My boyfriend tried to help me stand up, but I pushed him away.

I yelled at all the fuzzy shapes in my father's house. The shocked blurry faces looked back at me. I told them, "I can't pretend that he was something he wasn't anymore. The man you guys keep talking about died years ago. He left. He never came back." I pointed at my chest. "I never—he never met me." No one stopped me, so I called him a piece of shit, no good, good-for-nothing—I actually tried to take my shoe off and throw it at their wedding photograph on the mantle. That's when my boyfriend scooped me up. I tried to fight him, but my head spun until I threw up off the back porch, into the middle of the night like I owed it money.

The funeral the next day was hazy too. I remember lots of hugs and pats on the shoulder, but I don't remember anyone speaking to me.

I sound like a terrible daughter, like I hated him, but when everyone talked about him like a hero, like he was the craziest and bravest person they knew, I couldn't help but feel like I had been lied to or cheated somehow. Why did I only see him as a drunk, when so many saw him as a brother and friend, a dare-devil with a guardian angel, and a talented mechanic who never reached his potential.

There I was, just ready to bury him.

***

I think Janet's gonna analyze the shit out of that. In my peripheral vision, I see she is sipping on her second tea, trying to remember what her handbook suggests for a patient like me.

"Tell me about your boyfriend," Janet says.

"Hunter?" I ask.

"Sure, if that's his name."

I shake my head. I'm not ready.

She nods and changes direction. "How has your mother adjusted?

TRACK 17: "DRUNKEN POET'S DREAM"

My mother seemed fine, as if she'd been released from a prison she'd grown to accept. She cried when she talked about him, always in the same hushed voice, like she might anger his ghost. When she talked of what was next for her, she spoke loud and enthusiastic. She picked out color swatches to paint the house and called contractors to build a front porch. When she realized the Corvette was in the way, she abandoned the idea. She planned flower beds and priced repairing the fence, but the Corvette was in the way of those projects too. She finally listed it for sale but kept raising the price as if she didn't really want to sell it.

By July, she had started packing boxes. When the kitchen cabinets were empty, she finally told me she was moving back to California. Before I knew it, the house was empty. The only thing left was the garage: my dad's terrain.

Rainbows swirled in pans of motor oil in the driveway, like portals sprung from the gravel into the underworld. It was so hot I couldn't breathe. If I closed my eyes, I could convince myself a great weighted blanket soaked in sweat was draped over the holler.

My mom paced between a wall of boxes covered in my father's handwriting and a workbench littered with oily car parts and toolboxes. In the middle was an antique wooden toolbox I had given my father last Christmas. I remember he'd looked at it strangely and asked me, "Did you find this on the side of the road?"

"It's antique," I'd said. "Look at all the hidden compartments! Aren't they neat?"

He had grunted, discarded it on the floor, and returned to his cigarette and spiked tea.

When I saw it again in the garage, it was as if I was seeing it through my father's disappointed eyes. The wood was chipped and discolored by oil. The original grain had water damage. The handle was broken, so when you picked it up, it skewed to one side. Each drawer I tried to pull out, stuck half way. Only the largest compartment opened.

Inside were two empty pint bottles of whiskey. Well, at least he'd found a use for it, I thought. I'd lost count of all the bottles we'd found hidden around the house like Easter eggs.

Mom worked through the boxes on the opposite wall. She found my holiday Barbie dolls and slid them towards me.

"Why do we still have these?" I asked.

"They might be worth something," my mom said, just like she'd said the Christmas morning she had ripped them from my young hands.

A Barbie with a deep red velvet coat and gold gown stared out of the box at me. I picked her up, remembering the feeling the first time she was ripped from my hands. I had been admiring the white fur hat and collar, thinking they reminded me of rabbit fur. I'd never know how it felt against my fingers. "They'll be worth something one day," my mom had explained. Three more Christmases passed with gifts I could only look at. I tried to shove the stupid thing back into its box but it would only sit askew with its plastic face smirking back at me. I took all the Barbie dolls out of the box to reorganize them and found empty pint bottles scattered among paperback books.

To the Far Blue Mountains, one book said. The man on the cover looked somewhere off into the distance. His back was to me. His eyes were on the horizon. Arrows were stocked in his quiver. I thumbed through the pages. A photo of my mother fell out. She was in a bikini on a beach, smiling at the camera. She was beautiful, female, thin, muscular, and young, maybe in her late teens or early twenties.

"Mom?" I asked over my shoulder, "When was this?"

My mom came over. Tears gathered in her eyes, and she asked me how old I was.

"You don't remember how old your only begotten is?" I asked.

"I don't even know what today is," she said, looking back at the photograph. "But I know this was the day you were conceived."

"Gross." I recoiled.

"What?" She said, clutching the photograph to her chest. "Did you think your mother was a virgin and you were born of immaculate conception?"

"I did. I thought you were the Queen of Heaven. Who else holds a candle to your perfect reputation?"

"Hush."

"You're not the patron saint?" I feigned shock. "Our lady untier of knots?"

"Stop that."

"My whole life is a lie!" I threw my hand to my forehead like a bad theatre act.

My mother rolled her eyes and recited to me, "He without sin, Story; let him cast the first stone."

I pulled an empty pint bottle from the box. "That's the pot calling the kettle black."

My mother stood up abruptly, looking down at me like a child she should spank.

"Story, listen to me."

I felt the shift in the air, like a blanket had been pulled off. I rose to my feet and dropped the empty bottle of Ancient Age back on top of the paperbacks.

"I know I was the first to cast stones. To tell your father what kind of man I thought he was." She inhaled deeply. "I know you know I'm not perfect, Story."

"Mom, I was just joking—"

She persisted with her moral lesson. "Sometimes, we're wrong about more than we'll ever know. Did I ever tell you what the surgeon said, after your father's surgery didn't work?"

That night was a black hole. Fate had come and gone, leaving me standing in an empty hospital room. If she had told me then, it was lost to me now.

She said, "We all thought it would be his liver that would kill him. Every one of us accepted that, didn't we? We were so blinded by his faults, by how he inconvenienced us, and by how he shamed us. Never once did we check his heart. No one ever checked his heart." Her voice cracked. "But the surgeon who tried to save him—they said he had been suffering from heart failure slowly over the past year, possibly over several years."

"I'm sure drinking didn't help," I said, the words tasting like metal.

"Stop." She held her palm up to me. "This is not about what we think he should have done. The doctor said it was the fact that his liver wasn't fully functioning that gave him almost a year longer with us. Story, the doctor said his heart, in the condition he saw it, couldn't have supported a fully functioning liver." Her tears fell freely, then. The sun caught the dust in the air. She stood completely still, like a life-like portrait of a saint.

"I know he wasn't the greatest father," she said as if she could see the brick and mortar in my hands. "I know he hasn't been there for you like he wanted to be, like he always aspired to be, but you don't have to be angry with him anymore."

I acted as if she was gaslighting me, as if she was trying to make herself feel better, and I wouldn't have any of it.

She grabbed my shoulders and made me look her in the eyes. "Story, life comes from hard decisions. We will never know what someone sacrifices to stay a part of our lives. They'll never know what we sacrifice to be a part of their lives. If you focus on what they don't have, you'll miss what they do have—the best part of them, what they've kept for you."

***

I am crying. The tears feel like blood that coagulates to replace the scab I have picked. My splotchy face is akin to a scar with its fresh new skin shining with a brilliance that says *I survived this*. I know now, tears have healing power. In isolation, I am greedy with their power, crying whenever the fuck I feel like it.

I apologize to Janet nonetheless.

"You have nothing to apologize for."

"I know I haven't painted a very pretty picture of my father and now I'm sitting here crying, missing him, like I wouldn't hate him even if he came back."

"Sometimes grief is un-burying the memories that make you miss him, and sometimes grief is being angry he's not around to be mad at anymore."

"Or being mad that I'm walking in the footsteps of his ghost," I say.

Janet raises an eyebrow at me.

TRACK 18: "STEALING ELECTRICITY"

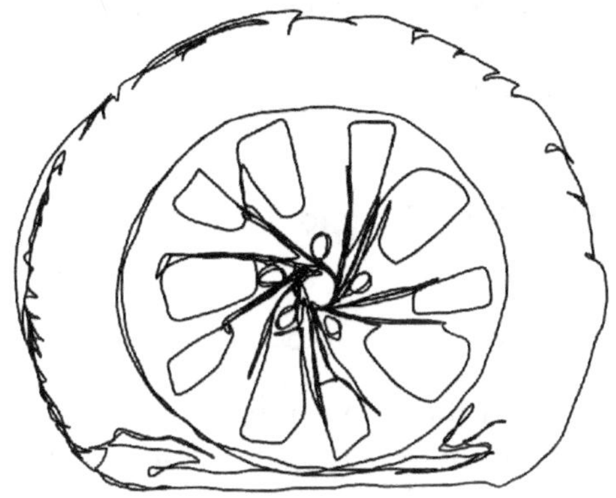

My mother tried to give me her house. It was a well-kept double-wide trailer, backed up to hundreds of acres of woods of the Daniel Boone National Forest. She didn't own the woods, just a narrow strip along the creek, far enough off the road to offer privacy. Dad's livelihood as a mechanic had junked most of the driveway and garage, but she did her best to keep it clean.

She told me, "I know you don't want to live out here, and you don't have to stay. I just thought if you didn't have rent, then maybe you could quit photographing weddings and take your time to find something else you love."

It was a very generous offer, but I told her no. I offered to help her finish cleaning it up so she could sell it.

"Why won't you let me do this for you," she asked me several times before she moved out for good.

I told her I didn't want to live alone. Jodie wasn't about to move out there with me, and I didn't know if Hunter and I were there yet in our relationship.

My mother took it upon herself to ask Hunter. Apparently, he had already been thinking about living with me but knew he didn't make enough money to pay rent for someplace nice. After my mom had brought it up to him, he recited to me all his own reasons: he could practice with his band because there weren't neighbors, he could save his money to put towards recording an album, he would wake up to me every day, and ideally, he could watch me walk around naked and we could have sex without muffling each other for the sake of roommates.

I asked him, "You're willing to drive an hour or more to gigs just so we can have loud sex?"

He said it was not a difficult question.

When Hunter and I took my mom to the airport, we told her we had decided to move in together, I would accept the house, and there would always be a place for her to come back to.

She smiled, patted my cheek, and said, "I knew you had some sense. Use some of that money you'll save to come see me."

It was strange living with Hunter in my parent's home. I mean, it was my home growing up too, but somehow it was hard to rectify the transfer of ownership. I was compelled to make up rules that would make it feel like my own, as if careless actions could cause us to fall into my parents' void. I didn't want to be my parents. I wanted a new role in the house.

We didn't cook, so the stove became storage. We put our bed in the living room. Hunter practiced with his band in my parents' room. My old room stayed empty. I left all the lights on all the time and cranked the A/C with the front door wide open.

Hunter didn't question any of it. He moved in with me like that was just how I lived. He just accepted that his band walked past me curled up in bed. He accepted that I left the windows open all night when it rained. He accepted that I refused to go into my parents' room. Most importantly, he accepted that, under no circumstances, ever, was he to touch or move the Corvette out front.

One long weekend in August, I had two weddings in Louisville back-to-back. That was eight hours just in driving time. The weddings went fine. I was in that already-put-in-my-two-weeks-notice mode, so even if they hadn't gone fine, it would have been fine. The problem was I was tired—physically, emotionally, and mentally. It was after midnight on Sunday when I finally came home.

I normally parked in front of the door, next to the Corvette, but Hunter had parked his van there to unload equipment into the house. Sleepily, I parked half in the dry, crunchy grass along the fence where the ragweed grew. I piled on the camera bags and tripods like I was bringing groceries into the house, cutting off circulation at my knuckles, wrists, and elbows.

When I made it inside the door, I dropped everything on the floor and barely kicked the door closed before I collapsed in bed with my clothes and my shoes still on. I woke up the next morning to Hunter's sneezes.

"Good morning," I said, still dressed in vendor attire. I got milk and cereal from the kitchen.

Hunter fought a sneeze while sitting on the couch with a roll of toilet paper in his hand. "Good morning," he said weakly, as if he had toilet paper shoved up his nose.

"Oh no, are you sick?" I asked him.

He shook his head as he blew his nose. "Allergies."

"Allergies to what?"

"Mold, pet hair, ragweed—" he started on a list and was interrupted by a sneezing fit. "Do you think there is mold in this house?"

"No," I said defensively.

"Like, have you checked it?"

"No," I repeated. "My mom was a neat freak."

He nodded, unconvinced. "But your dad wasn't."

"What are you trying to say?"

When he didn't respond, I returned to my cereal, and then, stopped "Wait, did you say ragweed?"

He nodded.

"I parked in the ragweed last night." I stood over the sink to look out the window. My car slanted haphazardly into the ditch along the driveway up to its side mirrors in weeds.

"Oh," he said, collecting more toilet paper, "then you came in and slept in your clothes. That's definitely—" Another sneeze.

I apologized but proceeded to defend myself. "I barely walked through it."

"That is precisely how pollen gets around." He said, and even as he said it, I could see his eyes were red. He gestured to me. "Could you at least change your clothes?"

I asked him, "Are you serious?"

"Yes." He sneezed. "Jesus Christ, do you not understand how allergies work. At least take your shoes off?"

I pointed out the open window in the kitchen. "I don't think taking my shoes off is going to help. Forgive me for stating the obvious but we are surrounded by ragweed. It's the fucking state flower. For my entire life, my parents have walked through ragweed and then this door and never taken off their shoes."

"Trust me," he said, snapping the window closed, "I can tell."

"What does that mean?"

He threw away his wad of toilet paper next to me. He asked me to get out of my clothes again.

I threw my shoulders back. How dare he insinuate my dead father was a slob. "Are you implying my family home just reeks of uncleanliness? This free house isn't clean enough for you? I'm not clean enough for you? My very presence is an attack on your physical wellbeing?"

"Will you calm down?" He asked with his hands raised in surrender.

I didn't realize I had my hand on my hip. I was fuming, and all he had asked was for me to strip out of my pollen covered clothing. I was my mother and father at the same time.

"Look," he said, "if no one ever suffered from allergies, then no one would have needed to take their shoes or coats off in this house. I get it. You and your family have walked these floors carefree. I'm jealous, if anything."

"Ah ha!" I yelled, "so the truth comes out! My family home is too disgusting for you. It is unclean! It is right up there with ungodly!"

"Jesus Christ, Story," Hunter yelled back at me, "No, I'm just fucking asking you to, for my sake, and for the love of God, please take your shoes off at the door. Please do not walk through the ragweed and then sleep in the bed—"

"Well, I wouldn't have parked in ragweed if you hadn't parked in my spot!" I interrupted him at a not entirely necessary volume.

He sneezed and then tried to take a deep breath. "Your spot? What are you five years old?"

It was déjà vu or the ghost of my mother when she was with my father, except I was my father, being insulted for being careless and irresponsible. I called Hunter a nag and mumbled angrily under my breath as I stormed out of the front door, slamming it behind me. I stalked to my car, kicking the ragweed to spitefully stir the pollen now that *I understood how it worked.* I pictured Hunter watching me, playing the role of my mother, but when I looked back towards the double-wide there was no one.

That made me even angrier. Petty thoughts flooded my mind. *How ungrateful he is! This isn't his house, it's mine! I ought to charge him rent! Fucking tell me to strip down at the front door because of the fucking ragweed.*

I wanted to storm off. I wanted to squeal tires. I didn't even have anywhere to go. It was an hour to the closest Walmart. The urge to display my anger was too much. I'd drive in circles if I had to.

I got in my car, started it and hammered on the gas to back up out of the ditch. It took a minute to realize I wasn't moving. I was ranting aloud to myself, to no one. The angry words poured forth from me like a swarm of bees as my car just spun in place.

Finally, I threw the door open and stepped back into the ragweed as my door bounced off the metal fencing along the ditch. I looked at the back tire; it was fine. I leaned around the driver side door to find a flat front tire. I knelt down in the ragweed, as if understanding how the tire had gone flat would somehow make me feel better. I found a broken fifth of whiskey—a friendly reminder that my father had been there. I held back tears as my shoulders rolled forward in defeat, and then, I began to sneeze.

I wanted to cry. I wanted to yell and curse my father's name, but I kept sneezing. It didn't stop until I managed to stand up and walk out of the ragweed. Even then, I must have sneezed so loud that Hunter came out the front door.

He was barefoot, wearing only his boxer briefs and leaning against the back of his van with his roll of toilet paper.

"Would you please get me a tire iron and a jack?" I managed to say, struggling to sound pissed off between sneezes.

He nodded and started towards the garage. I managed to tell him it was in the kitchen pantry, and he changed directions back into the house.

By now, the August sun was beating down on me. I was still in my black slacks and wrinkly white button up. I took off my shirt and threw it over the passenger side mirror. When Hunter came back out, he had put on pants. He whistled at me like he was suddenly in a better mood. He also carried a blanket, as if we were about to picnic.

Somehow that enraged me. He wasn't allowed to be in a better mood. We were fighting. He wasn't allowed to be the hero. He didn't get to save me. I needed to fix my own tire so I could storm off, dammit. I crossed my arms and watched him lay the blanket down and place the jack under the car.

"Of course, you would assume I can't change my own tire and I need a man to come save me because I'm so pitiful and helpless."

He sighed but didn't stop. The car's nose bucked up out of the ditch slowly, like a tired horse. Once the wheel was off the ground, he inspected the tire and the ground beneath it. He pulled out shards of glass, label and all.

"We'll be finding these for a while, won't we?" He said it with a smile.

"If you don't like it, you can leave," I said bitterly.

He sat the broken glass down on the blanket corner, ignoring me. "I'll find a weed eater and trim all this up," he said as he fitted the tire iron onto the lug nuts and spun the flat tire in the air.

"So, you can weed-eat, and change a tire in ragweed, but God forbid someone fall asleep in their shoes."

"I can wear a mask when I weed-eat."

I watched him fight the lug nuts on the free spinning wheel. I realized he didn't know how to change a tire.

He twisted the tire iron with two hands. At first, he tried to use the free rotation of the tire to jolt the tool in the opposite direction—the wheel just spun the other direction. I enjoyed watching him struggle, like a petty child.

"You're doing it wrong," I finally said. I pushed him out of the way and used the jack to lower the car back down. Once the flat tire was back on the ground, I used my full body weight to loosen the lug nuts by standing on one side and jerking up on the other.

"Get the spare," I said. The command felt like a role-reversal.

Hunter popped the trunk, pulled my spare tire out, and leaned it against the fence post. He asked me, "Did your dad teach you how to change a tire?"

I pumped the jack as I registered his words. Once the wheel was off the ground again, my fingers moved to the loosened lug nuts. Their chrome was cracked and sharp, not unlike my father. I told Hunter, "I remember being on the side of the highway. I was fourteen, and he was mad that I couldn't remember how to do it from the first time he'd told me. See, he always wanted a son. When he got me, I think he always thought he would just teach me all the same shit, and it'd be the same thing."

Hunter nodded at me with a smile, and I remembered that I was still mad at him. Somewhere, my father was very proud that his daughter was showing up a son, I thought.

I handed a lug nut to Hunter. The act confused me, like I was doing something wrong. When I looked at Hunter, he had an odd look on his face. I dismissed the feeling and turned to take the flat tire off. I hugged it, trying to lift it so I could slide it off the posts. It caught at every angle. My energy was draining, and I resorted to jerking each side. That's when I realized the car was moving. It rocked away from me. Then because of the incline of the ditch, it creaked back towards me.

It moved slowly, like a sinking ship. I would have had time to move out of the way, but I kept watching. I was entranced at how four tons of metal could fall in slow motion. It tricked my mind and made me think I could put a hand out and hold it.

Hunter's arms hooked around my waist, and he ripped me away toward the back of the vehicle where there was still room for two adults. We fell to the ground in the ragweed, our bodies warm and perspiring in the August sun. There was not a great crash, just a crunch like a potato chip bag being wadded up, as the front of my car folded its bumper around the spare tire, pinning it against the fence post.

My father's voice filled my ears, *Always block your wheels, Story! Always. Cars are meant to be on four wheels, just like horses need four legs. Do you know what happens to horses when they break a leg, Story? They get shot.*

Everything was fine, though. Hunter was slippery with sweat on top of me, like he could protect me from being crushed. Everything was fine. It could have been worse, but it was fine. My car would be fine, and we were both alive, not crushed like whiskey bottles.

"Are you okay?" Hunter asked me.

I really thought I was. I thought we had made it out unscathed.

"Story, you're bleeding," Hunter said, kneeling over me, inspecting my arm.

"No, I'm not," I said. "I think I'd know."

He brought his hand up in front of my face. The sun shone behind it. The blood covering his hand was a burgundy hue that only shadow could make.

I tried to sit up but my head spun and the pain receptors in my arm woke up to discover I had landed on pieces of my father's broken whiskey bottle.

***

Janet doesn't have to ask. I am already rolling up my sleeve to show her the scar above my elbow. I twist around in my seat completely, so she can run her finger along the lines where the skin is puffy and still pink, like a worm or a snake resting on top of the skin. I can only see the scar in a mirror, so I enjoy watching her face as she inspects it.

"Did you need stitches?" she asks me.

"Yes, fifteen," I say, watching her.

"How strange," she says. "I've never seen a scar like that."

"I know." I roll my sleeve back down. "Hunter liked to say it commemorated our first fight as a couple. We were officially over the honeymoon phase. He said we were on our way to getting a porch and rocking chairs."

I am talking too much. I am both smiling and crying. I miss him—I will miss him. I don't know why I feel so confused. He never wanted those things. It was just a snide comment made carelessly. I recoil back into my seat, like a serpent hiding in grass. I don't want to talk anymore. I check the time, and we still have more than an hour before landing. I think of sleeping, but I am on guard. The best I can do is pretend to sleep, and I suspect Janet knows the difference.

"Were you able to find a new job?" Janet asks out of the blue.

TRACK 19: "WORLD NEWS"

You could say I changed lanes very slowly. Jodie got me a job at her hotel. At first, it was just a day or two each week, because I still had weddings. I switched to full time by the fall. I went from making a couple thousand dollars in eight hours to making seventy-two dollars before taxes. It also meant I went from the person everyone turns to for answers to the person who folds laundry and collects complaints. I had gone from earning praise and verbal recommendations to reeking of nepotism. I was a pity hire.

For the most part it was blissfully boring. I mostly watched TV or read books. I was no longer responsible for the happiest day of other people's lives. The worst of the hospitality industry was noise complaints, overbooking, and well, the occasional sleepwalker.

On my first evening alone, Jodie tried to convince me nothing was going to happen. She had trained me all night, staying way past her normal shift. She was about to leave me for the evening. I'd be on my own for two hours before the night shift came in. She assured me it would be a slow night and I would get bored. I didn't like the idea of assuming nothing would happen. It felt like a jinx or a violation of Murphy's law.

When she left, everything was quiet. The lobby TV was on mute. The elevator was silent. The only thing I could hear, and only if I tried very hard, was the occasional semi on the highway. I paced for a few minutes.

Eventually, I pulled open my laptop and decided to edit photos from a wedding while I listened to music. I hadn't heard the elevator ding or seen the man enter the lobby. I noticed movement in my peripheral vision, and my gaze landed on the bare ass of a man rummaging through the newspapers.

I watched him cover himself with the front page of the New York Times. His hand cupped the paper around his body like he was wrapping delicate glassware. There was an image of a smokey sky on the front page, like an explosion. Just barely, I could make out the words *PLANE CRASHES IN SAN FRANCISCO*. I stared at the smoke in the image, a gray mass like a thundercloud. An image flashed in my mind like a strike of lighting—blue and electric. The grays and blacks morphed, rearranged, and became crumbling rocks.

The man bent over, putting his face where my gaze was, and said, "Excuse me, ma'am."

My eyes darted from his crotch to his face. His eyes darted from me to the glass-sliding door entrance. He slowly approached the counter, hiding his bottom half from me entirely. He told me he sleep-walked and had locked himself out of his room.

This was only my first day. I knew how to make keys, but I didn't know the procedure to confirm someone's identity who didn't have a photo ID ... or pants. I probably should have called Jodie, but she had faith that I could handle anything.

I stood at the computer with my fingers poised. "What is your room number?"

"210," he said.

"And your full name?"

"Greg Patterson. It says Gregory on my credit card."

There was in fact a Greg in 210, who's credit card said Gregory. That seemed sufficient to me, but something told me I should check everything I could; address, credit card digits, and phone number. What if this was just some ruse to get at the real Gregory? What if Gregory from 210 was in danger?

"Sir, can you give me your address?"

He spouted off his address so fast and automatic that I didn't catch it. "Excuse me, sir, speak slowly."

Greg was getting frustrated. He released one hand from his grip on the newspaper and slapped the counter. He apologized and spoke his address slowly and perfectly.

"Your phone number?"

"This is ridiculous," he said and then spouted off his phone number, credit card number, social security number and blood type. I decided any more questions would be ill-deserved torture for Greg. I slid a key into the machine, programmed it for 210, and slid it across the counter. Then, I watched as he waddled away with the newspaper crinkling, his bare feet slapping the tile, and the elevator politely welcoming him and carrying him away.

At first, I'd thought it had been humorous. I wanted to call Hunter and tell him what had happened. Then, I decided I ought to tell Jodie first and update her on any possible complaints from guests sighting a naked man in the hallway.

Then, I heard the elevator ding again.

Greg appeared, clutching his day-old news. His cheeks were red and his eyes fumed.

"The key didn't work," he said angrily as he approached the counter again.

I stumbled through my apologies, feeling too ashamed to look at him again. My fingers fumbled through the pile of cards. I had to make it twice because I accidentally pressed 221 instead of 210. When I extended the new card toward him, I didn't let my eyes quite reach his. Instead, my gaze rested on his arms. At his shoulders, I saw his chill bumps.

"Oh my God, you must be cold," I said. I rushed from the counter and ran into the back, still holding his key. There were several carts in the back. Some held dirty laundry, and some held clean laundry. Jodie and I had stacked all the towels on the bottom of one of the carts, but I couldn't find them. I heard a man scream. I looked up at the TV monitor that showed me the front desk. There was Greg, frozen in place, holding a hand out toward a figure walking through the glass doors. I saw him extend his arm.

I grabbed a bed sheet and ran to the front desk, having no clue what I was going to do. When I saw the scene, there was an older man shaking his cane at Greg and yelling in his raspy voice, "What in the hell's goin' on here? Who are you?" He turned on me and said, "Call the police!"

Greg was struggling to hold on to his news by this point, stumbling and fumbling with his hands and his words. "Sir, I'm so sorry, I'm so sorry, I was asleep. I walk—sleepwalk, sir—"

I panicked and tossed the sheet across the counter and over Greg like I was capturing a wild animal. The white sheet ballooned over him. It caught him unaware. Greg punched at it which made the older man raise his cane.

"He's a guest!" I yelled at the older man.

Finally, Greg poked his head out of the sheet and wrapped it around him. "Ma'am ..." Greg turned toward me. The older man squared off with him, still using his cane like a fencing sword. "Ma'am, if I could have my key?"

I was shaking by this point, cursing Jodie's name and her careless jinx on the night.

I had already lost it. I told him, "I'll make you a new one."

"You know this man?" the older man asked me.

For some reason, in my panicked state, I recited Greg's full name, his address, his phone number, and most of his credit card number, before Greg interrupted me.

"That's enough," he said. "This has been, by far, the worst experience." There was a crinkle of paper, and his hand peaked out of the sheet and placed the front page of the Times on the counter.

Just then, the glass doors slid open. An old woman emerged from the night dressed in a technicolor coat. Her gray hair flowed past her hips and her eyes smiled like a kid at Christmas. Betty was her name, and she laughed at all three of us. "What have we here? Sleep walking again, Mr. Patterson?"

"Yes, Ma'am," Greg said, kindly, nodding to Betty.

"I'm so sorry," I said, "Betty, I'm the new second shift and apparently the key machine is messed up."

"Oh sure," Betty said, wobbling her way around the older man, swatting down his cane. "The machine is the culprit, of course."

Betty patted Greg on the shoulder, crossed from the lobby to behind the front desk, and winked at me. She made another key and waved the men off with a friendly smile and a promise to discount their rooms.

"Jesus Christ," I said as I sank to the floor and buried my face in my hands.

She laughed at me for several minutes, patted me on the shoulder, and said, "The good Lord rarely gifts us with such pleasures as a man stripped naked and locked from his room. Let's not scare them off by saying his name in vain."

***

Janet is laughing so hard she must wipe her eyes with her shirt sleeve.

I laugh with her because enough time has passed that it is funny. Also, when you are laughing with someone, especially a stranger, you are compelled to keep it going. I tell Janet that Hunter still walks into our bedroom, naked, covered in only a sheet, and I repeat his full name, address, and credit card number.

I correct myself. "Well, he used to."

This brings back Janet's analyzing gaze.

We are both silent for a moment. The flight attendant appears from behind us in the aisle. I ask for a whiskey and Coke, and Janet gets a packet of cookies and milk.

"Did something happen between you and Hunter?" Janet asks as she dips her cookies in the milk.

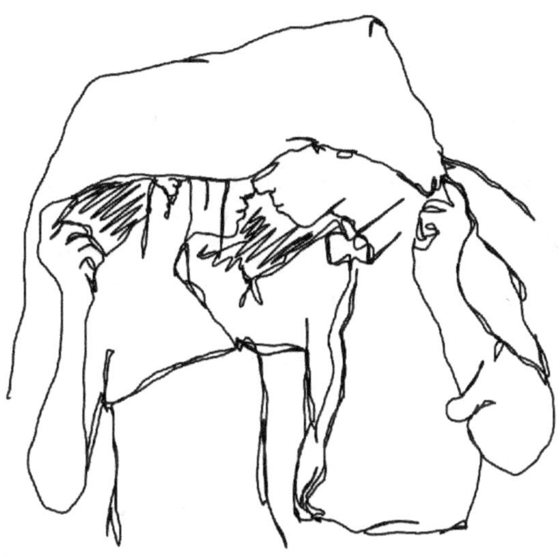

Nothing happened that I didn't see coming. I knew I wasn't a muse. I wasn't exotic or interesting, especially after I decided to quit photographing weddings. Neither one of us had to make money, so we didn't. That meant we didn't make enough money to move out of my parent's home. I think the universe didn't like to see adults have it so easy. Things kept happening to me.

Hunter invited me to a wedding with him. Admittedly, I was really excited. Being a vendor isn't like being a guest. If I ate the catered food, it was while standing and with guilt. I never got to enjoy an open bar. I never got to dress up. As a vendor, I was always genderless and soulless. I was never there to interrupt or disturb. I was an intruder in a natural habitat I brought nothing, left nothing, and took only photos with me.

He asked me to be his plus one back on Valentine's Day. This wedding was where I'd meet his family. The wedding was in early

September. Not quite summer but still warm and dry. The leaves were crispy green, starving for rain or death. I picked out a long corseted black dress with gold trim. It was strapless and shapely. I wore an arm cuff to hide the scab on my arm. My hair was long then. It was blond at the tips and chestnut at the roots. It was all very female, and looking female would be less conspicuous.

I can't remember who was getting married, a cousin maybe, but it was a big wedding. His entire family was there, and they all came at me at once.

"So, what do you do?" an aunt asked me.

"I'm a recovering wedding photographer," I joked.

"Oh, what do you do now?"

"I work as a desk clerk at a hotel."

"Oh," she said, looking me up and down. "Have you met Hunter's mother yet?"

"No," I confessed.

She smiled and walked off, distracted by another guest.

A cousin asked me, "So, you're a wedding photographer?"

I nodded.

"Is it hard to watch another wedding photographer? Are you, like, critiquing her? Does she use the same camera as you?"

"No," I said, "I'm very much enjoying being a guest."

The cousin thought this was uninteresting and abandoned me as well.

Hunter's mother, Susan, held her chin high as she looked disapprovingly at my dress. She said it was nice to meet me but in that obligatory way. I know, because she told Hunter he was handsome but did not tell me I looked nice. Isn't it common courtesy to tell someone they look nice when they are dressed up?

"Is this dress too much?" I asked Hunter when his mom excused herself to assist the florist.

"What do you mean?" He whispered back to me.

"Is it too revealing?"

He said I looked perfect, and he proceeded to introduce me as his nickname for me, Fish Sticks, so that certain people knew who I was in reference to stories he had told.

"Ohhh," they'd say with a chuckle, "Fish Sticks, right. Nice to finally meet you."

I couldn't tell if that meant they knew me as a friend, as previously married, or just as a fornicator from California.

One of Hunter's childhood friends Jaz was quick witted, self-deprecating, popular among the family, and flamboyantly kind. He was flattering and thought my move away from wedding photography must be the best decision of my life.

Hunter had left me in Jaz's care while he fixed his little brother's tie.

I asked Jaz, "So, what do I need to know about Hunter's family?"

"You'd have to be a saint to win their approval." Jaz said. We stood and watched as guests fanned themselves and waited in the shade of a great big oak for the ceremony to begin.

"I'm inappropriately dressed, then, yes?"

"I mean, it's a little ren-faire, but I love it. It's bold." Jaz had a way of saying things, it was so easy to believe him.

"I do look like a renaissance whore, don't I?" I asked, seeing myself from the perspective of someone who had never bought a pickle from a man in leather lace up boots.

Jaz called me darling and said I had nothing to fear. Hunter was going to love whoever he loved, and his mother knew it.

Just before the ceremony started, Jaz's plus one showed up, and I lost him to a dashing but quiet man who looked like he might lead everyone to the Red River Gorge for baptisms. He turned out to be the officiant.

For the portraits, Susan asked that Hunter and I stand off to the side with his father, a distracted but friendly man named Greg that I couldn't help but imagine naked with only a newspaper all day. Hunter's little brother was in almost every photo, whether the family liked it or not. When the family portraits were wrapping up, I watched as Hunter's mom stopped the photographer.

Oh no, I thought. Sure enough, she waved Hunter and Greg over to join her and her youngest son. She never gave me eye contact, so I kept my feet planted.

Hunter waved me over, but I said, "That's okay." His mother barely glanced at me and spoke loud enough for me to hear. "Just the family first, and then we'll add her in." Family first, then tramps.

I saw this all the time at weddings. A member of the family wanted a photo of only the ones that mattered. Sometimes it was a father or an aunt, but mostly it was mothers. Mothers protected the boundaries of the family at all cost.

"Mom, we live together," Hunter said, waving me over. He'd not seen the look in her eyes, as sharp as the scissors she would use to cut me out of the photo later. I didn't know what to do. I couldn't be as clueless as Hunter, so I stood on the end of their family and leaned out like an idiot, like a snag in carpet that you trim off to save your vacuum.

When his parents left, Hunter and I got drunk. It was our first wedding together, and we were learning so much about each other. One, we knew all the words to all the songs we hated. Two, neither of us could dance. We were two logs bouncing on the top of the water, impeding the path of agile guests. Lastly, we found this to be intoxicatingly hilarious.

I loved not being the wedding photographer but still knowing what kind of photograph was being taken and how to evade it. The hired photographer never used a direct flash, which meant she couldn't capture a body in high-speed motion. I played a game. If I saw her camera point towards me, I would spin. My long hair would whip around and obscure my face. I saw the photos later; I was just a blurry figure, like Hunter had danced with Sasquatch. After Susan cut me out of her family portrait, there would be no record of me at that wedding.

Everything was going well until the sparkler send-off. I hated sparklers. Every wedding photographer did. Don't be fooled by their fake smiles and their forced enthusiasm. They were acting. They didn't want them. No sane person wanted the participants of an open bar to be in charge of large sticks with tiny explosions over their head.

Hunter and I were standing near the end of the line of groomsmen stripped down to their untucked shirts and beltless dress pants. The bride and groom walked back and forth a half-dozen times, trying to perfect the magazine-cuddle-and-walk and the movie-star-kiss-and-dip. These were the good sparklers, they lasted long enough to grow bored. The inebriated groomsmen started sword fighting too close to me.

"Fire!" Jaz yelled, pointing at me.

Someone threw their beer on me. Hunter slung his jacket over my head. Between the two actions, the flames were extinguished quickly, but the damage had been done. I was humiliated. Finally, I had been both highlighted and concealed. I was now the most exciting part of someone else's wedding and the face no one would remember.

"Is she okay?" I heard a half dozen times.

"Poor thing."

"Was she standing too close?"

"Hairspray is so flammable."

I stayed hidden under Hunter's coat. He navigated me away from the guests, lifted the flap of his jacket, and joined me underneath it. Illuminated by the light of his phone, he asked if I was okay.

"How do I look?" I asked.

"You look beautiful," he said, with a kiss on my forehead.

"Don't flatter me," I said, beginning to cry.

"Can we take the coat off and have a look?" he asked. I let him. He cocked his head to the side, and finger-combed my hair over. "You know what?" he said, taking a step back, "It kind of looks good. Smells terrible, but looks good."

Jaz appeared on one side of him and the officiant appeared on the other. They looked me up and down, all with the same obtuse angle to their necks. They were three silhouettes against the dying sparklers behind them. Their faces were illuminated by only their phones.

Hunter said I looked like a warrior.

"Half Alexander the Great," the officiant said.

"Half Xena, Warrior Princess," Jaz added, with a big smile on his face.

Each statement felt like a prophecy: the spinning, measuring, and cutting off of the thread of my fate. I blinked them away until the image of sparklers faded like a lens going out of focus, filling the frame with star shaped bokeh before I passed out.

***

"You are divorced?" Janet asks, completely unconcerned with the tragedy of my hair.

I nod.

She is nodding to herself.

"What?" I ask.

"Some things make sense to me now," she says.

"Like what?" I orient myself towards her. I am not sure if I am armed to fight off her theories or soak them in fully.

"Do you think it's possible that you do not trust the feelings of others?"

"I trust people."

"But do you trust their feelings?"

I need further clarification. "Are you asking if I believe their feelings are trustworthy?"

"Not quite," she says. Together we have boxed in the space between us. Whatever passes between us will not escape. "Do you believe that those around you ... love you?"

"No," I answer with a certainty that is unfamiliar on my tongue.

TRACK 21: "ELVIS PRESLEY BLUES"

I am a cursed, soulless shell. I'm a well of darkness covered over with a piece of plywood, covered over with garden dirt, and sewn with seeds that blossom sporadically and are plucked by kin and strangers alike. No one knows of the danger beneath them. No one knows my true nature ... except Elvis, apparently.

Not long after the wedding, Hunter took his younger brother, Simon, and me to the county fair. The air smelt like funnel cakes, gasoline, and dying foliage. It came at me through the car window like the hot breath of a secret against my ear.

Simon was a sassy eight-year-old. I had offered to let Simon sit up front, but he gave me a look from under his eyebrows. "Do you want me dead? I can't sit up front yet. I'm only eight."

When Hunter parked the car in the field outside the fairgrounds, he lit a cigarette. I waited for Simon to comment on Hunter's cancer sticks or terrible tragic death, but he grabbed Hunter's free hand and pulled him towards the fair, unconcerned with me.

"Let's start with a fair burger, what do you say?" Hunter asked him with a glance over his shoulder at me as I trailed behind.

"I want a bunny," Simon declared.

"Well, that's a strange burger but I'll see what I can do."

"No!" Simon said, "A live bunny."

Hunter looked back at me with his forehead furrowed. "Bubby, I don't think mom wants a bunny in her house."

"Let me handle mom," Simon said, like he was the professional at handling moms.

We found bunnies at a carnival game with dozens of red Solo® cups around a single one on a pedestal in the center. Simon paid the game operator who dumped a bucket of ping pong balls into a basket at the tent's edge. We watched Simon spend $40 trying to land one in the center cup. When he was offered the prize of a fish, he asked, "how many fish will equal a bunny?"

The game operator shook his head.

Hunter spoke gently to Simon. "How about I take you to a pet store tomorrow. Save your money."

"Just one more? Will you try it?" Simon's eyes glistened with moisture.

Hunter caved. "Okay, but this is the last one. We're taking Story for her first fair burger next."

Simon danced on his toes, holding his breath as Hunter started in on his bucket load of shots. As the ping pong balls dwindled down. Simon got desperate. "Wait, let me blow on it!"

That didn't work.

"Let me rub it between my fingers!" he said. Then, he turned accusatory. "Did you pray? You have to pray!"

Finally, it was down to the last one. Simon had run out of ideas for good luck. He kept looking at the cage of bunnies like he wasn't ready to say goodbye, like he might steal one if it came down to it.

"I know," Hunter declared, "Story!" He pushed the white plastic orb in my face. "A kiss?"

"No," I said with a step back.

"Please?" Hunter cooed. "Nothing is as magical as your kiss. I know it will work."

I looked from Hunter to Simon. The eight-year-old was not pleased by this turn of events. There was no part of him that wanted a bunny if it was won by my lips. If his god or brother couldn't get the bunny for him, then he didn't want it. And if he didn't get the bunny because my kiss didn't work, his misery would be all my fault.

"Please don't put this on me," I whispered to Hunter.

"It's just a game." He laughed. "It's all in good fun. We'll get him a bunny tomorrow."

I believed him. I pressed my lips to that disgusting ping pong ball, and I prayed that Simon would forgive Hunter and me. Hunter tossed it.

Plop.

"Well, I'll be a son of a—" Hunter said, as he slipped a cigarette into his mouth, like he had just won a gun fight in a western movie. Simon was so moved by the surprise he completely forgot that I had anything to do with it. He hugged Hunter violently. Then he picked out a rust-colored bunny. The game operator tossed the furry thing into a cardboard box and handed it over.

We walked in loops around the fair, eating our fair-burgers and brainstorming names for the bunny.

"Tom." Hunter had resorted to single syllable suggestions after Simon had turned down his best: Scarlett O-Hare, Rabbit De Niro, and Pickles.

"No! That's a person's name," Simon explained.

"Cow," Hunter said, an Ale-8 in his hand. "You've turned down all my best work, I'm fresh out of ideas. Maybe Story has some good ideas."

Simon didn't even look at me. He checked on his bunny in the box and nearly ran into two plump and chatty women. They stood at the end of a line behind two young boys in swim trunks and T-shirts with their hands full of cotton candy. At the front of the line was a couple in Realtree® print. The man had his hand on a slanted surface, and the woman was smiling around the straw of a milkshake.

The attraction looked like an arcade penny machine or a booth that should have had glass walls around an animatronic Elvis Presley bust that would come alive and tell you your fortune. It wasn't convincing by any means. I could detect the folds of the cardboard frame like the whole contraption accordioned into a suitcase. The animatronic Elvis Presley was a real man, who after the chiming of music, jerked to life and raised his head to face the man in Realtree® print.

"You may be camouflaged, but the King sees all," Elvis said. He continued in a broken rhythm, like the words were being computer generated. "The King advises that you should use caution with whom you fall in love. While love is grand ..." He motioned dramatically with jerking movements and a shifting gaze. "... divorce is ten grand ... or more."

The man in the Realtree® print laughed, and the woman with him snorted her milkshake onto the ground.

"Now, take your fortune ..." Elvis continued, pulling a card from beside the man's hand and passing it to him. "... and enjoy your time at the fair."

Then, as if the credits had run out, the King bowed his head and closed his eyes.

The two young boys next in line were hesitant about the sleeping machine.

"Go on. Shit or get off the pot," one of the older women said.

The shorter of the two boys placed his hand on the platform.

"Ah, the King can see your deepest desires. You desire knowledge about the ladies."

The boy recoiled his hand like he had stuck it down a crawdad hole.

"Listen closely, and the King will reveal all there is to know. First, ladies are simple," Elvis began. "Yes means yes, and no means no." He paused. His animatronic-like hand pointed at the young boy. "But sometimes ..." His face turned to confusion. "... yes means no, yes means maybe, and maybe means no." Elvis held up two fingers. his straight composure faltered while the boys giggled. "Second, always hold a door open for a lady." Elvis held both hands up. "But don't feel bad when they say, 'What? You don't think I can't open my own door?'"

The adults giggled, but the kids wore confused looks.

"Lastly," he said, "if you want to know how to please a woman, just talk to a neuroscience major from Columbia University. Now that you know all there is to know, please take your fortune and enjoy your time at the fair."

The boy snatched his fortune card and practically ran off with the two older women.

"Go on." Hunter elbowed me toward Elvis. "Let's see what your fate is."

"You go," I said, unwilling to take a step closer.

"I already know my fate, babe. My future is with you." Hunter winked.

"Gross," Simon interrupted. "I want to leave."

"Go on," Hunter told me. "We'll loop around and come back." He looked to Simon. "And maybe we'll have a bunny name by then."

I figured I could stand some time away from Simon's glare. Hunter winked at me again, and they disappeared into the crowd.

I turned to Elvis and placed my hand as the other two had. My hand fit perfectly in the outline made by sparkling, red glue. I was looking at the way the fingers of the outline had the same knotty knuckles as mine when it dawned on me that I hadn't heard Elvis wake up. He was still asleep, more shadowed than I remember. I hit the button, again.

Nothing. *No fortune for me,* I thought. *No interesting bits to feed off of for me.*

Just as I was about to give up, a jingle of notes echoed from a fuzzy speaker.

"Ahhh!" Elvis started, and his voice cracked and buzzed. "I see your deepest—" His hands and eyes jerked as if the recording skipped. "The King knows—the King sees—"

This made no sense, because he was a real person. He was a living, breathing man, except broken.

Suddenly, the volume and clarity returned but not to his familiar robotic manner. Instead in a perfect impersonation of the King himself, Elvis began to sing "You're the Devil in Disguise."

I stared at Elvis—the man, the conjurer, and the machine—as he continued his routine and returned to his stone-faced and robotic act. "Please take your fortune and enjoy your time at the fair."

Elvis dropped the card next to my hand, bowed, and closed his eyes. Curtains fell all around him like he was turned off, lowering the veil so that none of my questions could be answered. I opened the curtains to look inside but found nothing but darkness. I snatched the small card with my fortune on it and read the words:

> *According to legend, the person that could undo the Gordian Knot would rule all of Asia. Instead of untying it, Alexander the Great took out his sword and cut through it in a single stroke. You too will find unique solutions to problems.*

I was on my way around the cardboard booth to accost an Elvis impersonator when Hunter grabbed my shoulder.

"Looking for the strings and pulleys?" He asked.

"Did you hear him?" I asked.

He looked confused. "No, what happened?"

I just stood and stared at him, unwilling to profess the words from my own mouth, *he called me the devil.* The words piled up in my throat like a crowd of people rushing to the exits when someone yells fire inside a building. The weak were trampled. The doors wouldn't open. They all burned up, turning to ash.

Hunter frowned at me.

I forced out a laugh. "Nothing. Sorry, I think I zoned out a bit."

Suddenly, the rush of the fair hit my ears all at once—the music of the Ferris wheel, the screams of kids on rides, the popping of balloons, the grinding of gears and jolting of bumper cars, the revving of engines, the buzz of mosquitos, and the echo of an announcer introducing the start of the demolition derby.

"Guess what." With his hand around my shoulder, he steered me towards Simon, who actually smiled when he looked back at me.

Simon chirped, "We picked out a name."

Hunter beamed at me and then motioned to Simon. "Well go on. Tell her."

Simon said, "Elvis!"

***

"You don't strike me as someone who is superstitious," Janet says.

"This isn't superstition. This is fate," I say.

Janet leans back into her chair. "You believe you are the devil?"

"Of course not," I say, but I don't know how to explain it. It's as if I'm looking for words that don't exist. It's a gut feeling. It's dread. It's the reptilian part of my brain that has evolved over hundreds of thousands of years to keep me alive. If I talk about certainty in the realm of fear, I'm paranoid. If I talk about signs, I'm a crazy person.

It's being the only person who knows the kind of truth that is buried in the meat of my bones and between the synapses of my brain. It's been there all along, from the moment of conception.

TRACK 22: "DRINKIN' IN MY SUNDAY DRESS"

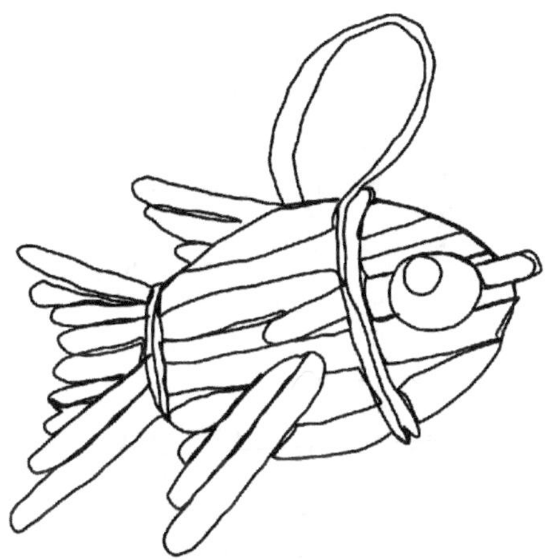

I am my father's daughter. My father fixed cars because he broke them. Destruction was his creative outlet. His life was spent repairing cracks and leaks, spilling oil and blood, and drinking sweat and antifreeze. His heart depended on the breaking of his liver. This world knows me by the man that preceded me.

Three days ago, Hunter invited me to his family's home. I was under the impression it was just a family dinner. Hunter grew up in a nice home. Not big-city nice, but rural folk nice. It had brick veneer, shutters around the windows that all matched and weren't falling off, and a big, well-manicured yard that was decorated for Christmas in the classiest way possible while still going over the top. A doormat played a midi version of *Jingle Bell Rock* when we stepped up to the front door. The catchy tune interrupted my mental practice of Hunter's mother's name. *Susan. Not Suzanne. Suuuusan.*

Simon answered the door. He was dressed as an elf. "Oh, you," he said grimacing.

Greg appeared, behind him, bright and cheery, holding a newspaper in his hand. "You all caught me reading the news!"

A flashback to a sleepwalker inspired an inappropriately robust laugh from me.

"Still?" Hunter whispered.

Greg, blissfully unaffected, asked Simon to let Susan know we had arrived.

By the time Hunter and I had taken our shoes off, Susan found us in the kitchen. She asked Hunter, "Why didn't you tell us you were bringing a guest?"

"I did," Hunter said, hugging her back.

"You most certainly did not."

"I didn't?" Hunter asked, "I could have sworn I did."

Susan sighed without any effort to conceal it. I received a cursory smile, and she said she had to rush off to set another place at the table. I could have rung Hunter's neck.

"No problem. There's always plenty of food," Greg said to me, as he shimmied behind us and motioned for us to follow him.

In the vaulted living room, every crevice and corner was decorated. Forget Hallmark or the movies. The inside of this house had plywood cut out store fronts. It smelled like a forest coated in cinnamon rolls. There was a hot chocolate urn on an ornate rolling cart by the entrance. The shelves on the walls, inside the arches of the store fronts, were filled with jars of multi-colored candy. In the middle of the room was a fake plush campfire with log-shaped pillows. Next to it, there was a tray of chocolates, marshmallows, and steaming mugs, surrounded by four rocking chairs. Not five.

Their Christmas tree must have been eight feet tall. Its branches drooped with ornaments, strings of popcorn, and twinkling lights. There were presents stacked high enough to hide the bottom third of it and presents still overflowed into a fireplace off to the side, where the bottom half of a stuffed Santa was suspended. The floor was carpeted in a plush white rug, like snow fall. From the ceiling hung snowflakes and robins with ribbons, as if they were tying bows on the store fronts, like it was fucking Cinderella on Ice.

The only word I could manage was, "Wow."

"It's a little extravagant," Greg said, "but Simon won't be young forever. Hunter certainly grew up too fast."

"You guys are like parents of the year," I said.

Greg beamed and described how he had constructed the store fronts until Susan called for everyone to go to the dining room.

We ate a pot roast and mostly listened to Simon choose the topic of conversation. It was nice having a chatty eight-year-old at the dinner table. The adults seemed content letting him steer the conversation. It was Simon Says. The game allowed Susan and Greg to politely ignore me. Who would interrupt the charismatic and eloquent child to find out anything about the new person at the table? Of course, I'm sure they already knew everything they needed to know from Hunter.

I went to salt my potatoes. I wasn't paying attention, and grabbed the first white granular shaker I saw. The first words were spoken to me since we'd sat at the table.

"Sugar on your potatoes?" Susan asked.

I didn't know what she was talking about. I thought it was the strangest string of words I had ever heard. Then, I looked down and registered the sugar dispenser.

The room burst into laughter, including Simon. Susan offered me more potatoes, barely containing her smile.

Hunter shrugged. "Nothing about you surprises me anymore," he said as he laughed. I ate those potatoes. I thought wasting them would look worse. I didn't want their memory of me to be, *she came in and sugared the potatoes and threw 'em away.* Instead, I was the grown woman who accidentally sugared her potatoes and ate them like a dare.

When dinner was over, Greg stood up and pointed at me, "I need a strong beverage. How about you?"

I perked up quickly. I told him, "I would like that very much."

He shook his finger at me, grinning, and said, "I thought you looked like the night owl type. Usually it's just Hunter and me."

I looked at Hunter, and he winked at me.

"How do you like it fixed?" he asked as he stepped into the kitchen and opened a cabinet above the sink.

"On the rocks," I said.

Susan dropped her fork, and Greg cleared his throat. Hunter stifled a laugh and shook his head.

Then, Simon looked at me, for the first time all night, with genuine interest. "You put rocks in your coffee?"

I stared back at him, registering his confusion. My own confusion reflected back at me ... *coffee, not bourbon, he offered me coffee.*

Greg pulled a coffee mug out. "That's my fault," he said. "There are several kinds of strong drinks. I should have been clearer. You won't find any alcohol in this house."

"Oh," I said as my cheeks got hot. I volunteered information like it was my last defense. "Yeah, at my house bourbon is for dessert. Well, it used to be." The room was silent and tense. "Black. I like my coffee black."

Greg nodded at me as he got the coffee maker going. The sound of gurgling hot water over coffee grounds filled the ensuing silence until Simon spoke. "Can I have my milk with rocks."

"It's *on the rocks*," Hunter corrected him.

"Hunter!" Susan snapped.

Hunter laughed. "I just want him to be well-informed."

Susan stood and suggested we move to the living room, so that's what we did.

"Story," Susan said to me from one of the rocking chairs, "some of the ornaments on that tree are 70 years old. They came from my grandmothers. Our yearly tradition is for the boys to get new ornaments to put on the tree."

"That sounds really sweet," I said, still standing with Hunter in the doorway.

"Seventy years of ornaments make for a very full tree," Hunter said.

"We keep buying bigger and bigger trees," Greg chimed in as he handed me a steaming cup of black coffee.

"If we had known you were coming," Susan said, "we would have suggested you bring one."

This was the first instance of Susan insinuating there would be any memorialization of my intrusion. I was surprised and honored. I was so starved for attention and inclusion that even this errant comment made me feel like the evening hadn't been a waste. Maybe she even liked me.

Then, Hunter piped up. "I brought an ornament for Story."

Susan and Simon's heads swiveled like snowy owls.

"That's great!" Greg said, handing a coffee to Hunter. "Let's see it!"

Hunter pulled the ornament from the pocket of his coat, which hung by the door. When he dangled it in the air, I could finally see it was a fish made of popsicle sticks—*fish sticks.*

"Simon, can you help Story put her ornament on the tree?" Hunter asked.

"No," Simon said, as if he was asked whether or not he wanted broccoli.

"Simon," Susan said an octave lower than her normal pitch.

"I don't want to," Simon said, from his place at the stuffed campfire. "That's *our* Christmas tree. She's not a part of our family."

The room filled with an uneasy tension, like Christmas lights strung tightly across the yard as tripping wire, booby-trapped defenses against the unwanted. *Merry Christmas, but stay out.*

The illusion of joy and peace fell apart. Susan and Greg stumbled over their words to excuse their son and to make me feel welcome. Hunter looked at me with a look that said, *kids say the craziest things.*

Susan rose from her chair and crouched by Simon. "Honey, this year we are inviting Story to celebrate Christmas with us."

"Yeah buddy," Greg said, joining Susan and Simon. "It's just for this year." He cleared his throat. "I mean, maybe next year too. … Not that they're getting married, or anything—not that they aren't!"

"Greg," Susan said, as if his name translated to *Period: full stop, end of sentence.*

"Woah." Hunter laughed deeply as if he were terrified. "It's just popsicle sticks, people." Hunter handed me the ornament. "Maybe it will be more fun if Story picks her own spot."

I just stared at him like he'd asked me to cross an alligator infested moat.

"Go on, Story," Greg said. "Pick you out a spot near the top."

Every direction was the wrong direction. I was eating sugared potatoes again. Simon stared at me as I inched my way across the white plush floors, past the candy-laden walls, beneath the robins and their red bows.

It was just me and the tree. I maneuvered my feet between gifts and craned my neck to see to the top. The tree filled my vision; a lumpy clay snowman read *Hunter 1994*; a plastic baby rattle read *Baby's first Christmas*; a perfect figurine of Boba Fett paired with an illuminated lightsaber read *Hunter 1997*; a porcelain bunny read *Simon, 2013.*

Further in were more layers, like rings of a tree. Glass ornaments so old that their paint was translucent. Their painted lines were cracked like a warm breath might melt them off. There were painted ornaments of places I knew and some I didn't—a drive-in theater, the Red River Gorge, Nada Tunnel. They were the backdrops to angels, the baby Jesus in the manger, all three wise men and their camels, and the star of Bethlehem.

There were ornaments of every shape and size, from every generation of Christmas tree trends—teardrop-shaped, egg-shaped, icicles, lamp-shaped, and spheres. They were made of glass, porcelain, wood, fabric, plaster, and gourds. There was silvery tinsel and garland made of popcorn, construction paper, dried leaves, orange-slices, and braided yarn. The tree was its own ecosystem of mementos, like a time capsule on display.

Simon was right. I wasn't part of this. The fish shaped popsicle sticks in my hand stunk of a foreign upbringing, foreign faith, and foreign matter. I was an invasive species, like a honeysuckle vine. I was fish sticks, greasy and artery clogging. I was my father's daughter. A wet sinner.

It pained me to extend my hand towards the tree, placing the ornament on the very tip of a branch. The ornament swayed gently, as if looking left and right before crossing a road. Then it stabilized and the tree was still standing. Lightning didn't strike it.

I stepped back, and it was all there.

I turned to face Hunter and his family and was greeted with three smiles—one small, one medium and one large. Simon frowned. His tiny little eyebrows met in the middle. I couldn't tell if it was confusion or anger. It was gone too fast. I watched as the small features of his elfish face morphed into fear.

Susan gasped. Her hands snapped to her mouth.

Greg's arms lurched towards me, as if to catch something that I hadn't thrown yet.

Hunter raised both arms like he was shielding his head, or telling me to shield my head.

I imagine the fall began very slowly. That eight foot Christmas tree —the beacon of Hunter's family, their yearly sentinel, adorned with every single scrap of memorabilia, carefully decorated and worshiped with the correct liturgy and reverence—came crashing down on top of me. It took me to the ground. It showered me in singing music boxes, porcelain baby shoes, hardened Play-Doh guitars, and vacation Bible school yarn crosses. I was buried in Hunter's past and present in an instant, foreshadowing any future I had with him.

***

Janet thinks I am funny. She is trying very hard to conceal her laughter, and it is unbecoming.

"I'm sorry," she says, finally letting an airy laugh escape her nose. She waves her hand in front of her face and fills her lungs. "I am so sorry."

I bite my lip, because I want to see the humor in it. I want to see something other than my faults and ultimate doom, but I cannot.

"Okay," she says. "I know it seems like a personal attack on you, but sometimes, trees fall. And for the record, no one knows how to win the heart of an eight-year-old. If you focus on these things, you will drive yourself crazy trying to figure out why it all happens."

I am not satisfied with this answer, and Janet knows it.

"I don't know much about your divorce, but I'm divorced. I was in survival mode when my spousal relationship failed. My trust was broken, so I was very hesitant to trust again. Add that to your tense relationship with your late father and you have accumulated several years of having members of your support system let you down. I think it's possible you fear a rejection that isn't coming."

Laughter burst from me. I am shaking my head. Janet doesn't know anything.

TRACK 23: "DON'T KISS ME GOODBYE"

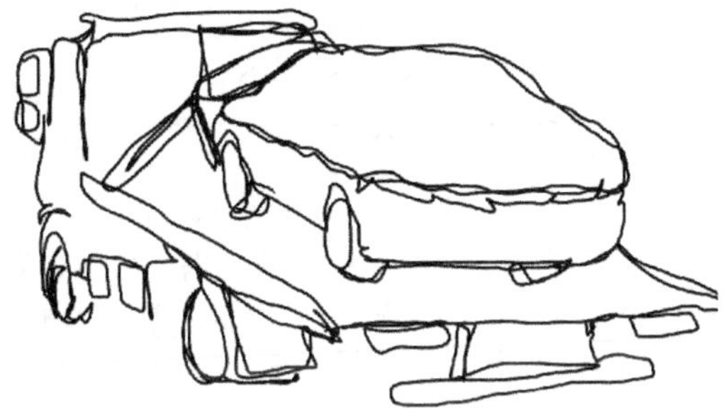

My car blew up that night. I hadn't changed the oil. How's that for irony?

It happened in the middle of nowhere. Hunter and I were taking the long way home. I was feeling hopeless, and he was deep in thought. He pulled over to look out at a coal wash nestled in a crook of the Kentucky river. We smoked cigarettes and stared at a super moon reflected in the still water surface. When he went to back up, the car sputtered, grinded pistons, and died.

The tow truck said it would be a two-hour wait. I had pleaded with Hunter not to call his mom, so we waited inside the metal carcass not talking about how it was getting colder and colder by the minute.

"Car trouble aside, I thought dinner went well," Hunter said to me.

"Before or after I ruined Christmas?"

Hunter laughed and shook his head. "How bizarre. A brand-new Christmas tree and one of the legs break."

"I'm just not cut out for meeting the family," I said. "And Simon, man, I think he might plot my murder if Susan would let him have a smartphone."

Hunter laughed. "Don't be too hard on yourself. My family will come around."

I was thrown. I had almost thought his mom and dad were already around. I mean, Greg had always welcomed me with open arms, and Susan had told me to come back anytime. I thought I had finally made it. It was just Simon left.

But of course, that was probably just my brain damage from their Christmas tree. Of course they were just being nice. No one had come around. If they had, I would have felt comfortable letting Hunter ask them for help. He would have insisted we call them instead of the tow truck.

"I can't afford to care what your family thinks of me," I said as I lit a cigarette.

"Woah," he said. "You're being a little dramatic. Aren't you?"

"No," I said. "Dramatic is freaking out when a grown woman wants a glass of bourbon instead of coffee. That's dramatic. I'm sorry I didn't grow up in a Disney movie."

He tossed a spent cigarette out and lit another one. "Oh, are we insulting my family now?"

Something primal emerged within me, and it felt cornered. Wild rage filtered my words. "No, really, what do I have to do to earn a spot on your family's Christmas tree, without tearing the damn thing down?"

The tears fell from my eyes like desperate souls jumping from a burning building.

"What is this really about?" he asked me point blank.

I took a deep breath and tried to think about the words I meant to say, the words I wanted to say. He was silent and impossibly calm and resilient. How was he so calm? How had so much happened in one night, and he was still a rock? I was the vodka, and he was the rocks. He was the chill to my burn. An iceberg. An island. A haven. I desired only him. I feared only losing him.

"Would you marry me?" I asked.

Hunter's eyebrow quirked like it was a joke. "Like, hypothetically?"

"Like right now."

He didn't respond right away, so I slung my car door open. The cold night air hit me like a wall, and it was snowing. I sprinted around the front of the car, opened his door, and got down on both knees, clasping his free hand. His other hand held a forgotten cigarette that was more ash than tobacco.

"Marry me," I said. "I have never once doubted whether I was supposed to be with you. From the moment I met you, I knew how much it would hurt to lose you."

He still didn't respond.

"I thought I'd never want to get married again. I thought I'd never risk losing a part of myself for anyone else. I'm sorry I don't have a ring. But I'll take my shoes off at the front door, and I'll handle the yard work so you don't have to. Just … marry me."

He tried smoking, but his cigarette had gone out. He tossed it. He stepped out of the car and pulled me up to my feet. I watched snowflakes fall onto his hair and shoulders like tiny little webs failing to capture him—melting upon impact.

"Story," he said, soaked in regret, like my name came with an unhappy ending.

I ripped my hand from his grasp and stepped away from him.

"Wait," he said.

"You're saying no?" I asked.

"Give me some time," he said.

"Time? Time to talk yourself into it?"

He laughed and released my hands. He shrugged and waved around. He could barely force out a full word.

Two bright headlights appeared, blinding and relentless. The sound of the tow truck was violent and abrupt, and I don't know how I hadn't heard it before. It shuttered to a halt, sliding in the gravel. The driver side door flung open, and a short man with light colored hair and a neck tattoo emerged looking like he'd gone through hell and back.

"It's a bad night for car trouble folks. I hope you're not going far." The man looked barely older than a kid. He still had an air of rebellion and immaturity about him. Hunter and I met him with silence. We were both recovering from the whiplash of this new character inserted into the conversation.

He stared back at us and smiled at me. He looked at Hunter, and his smile faltered. By the time his gaze returned to me, his smile was gone.

"No use wasting time. There's a goddamn snow storm about to hit," he said and got back in his tow truck. Hunter tried to grab my hand, but I stuffed it in the pocket of my coat. I watched the tow truck maneuver towards my car, registering the sounds of shifting gravel, the piercing decibels of its reversing beep, and the screech of brakes like metal on metal.

The horizon was lost to me. All I could see was snow. It fell and gathered into thick piles on the ground, on my car, and on my shoulders.

As if the night had been challenged in a bet, I felt the moist, warm drip of my period between my legs, soaking into my underwear. I said nothing. I did nothing. I piled into the cab and rode in the middle between a silent Hunter and the driver who volunteered his opinions about how he didn't have a problem with women but they didn't have no right to be his boss. He worked too hard to be told what to do by a woman.

What should have been a forty-five-minute ride home took two hours. The storm had come on fast and no one had predicted how bad it would be. The kid steered the tow truck along the back country roads, never going faster than a crawling speed. We passed a half-dozen stranded cars at a time.

In my exhaustion and defeat, I was surprised by a feeling of invincibility. Is this what rock bottom felt like? If this was the worst the world could throw at me, then maybe I could survive anything. My car had died, Hunter had rejected my marriage proposal, and a sexist man-child was our savior, but the lining of my uterus was shedding. Blood was soaking through my pants and smearing its destructive and creative power all over the upholstery.

I would leave a mark, and maybe that's all I ever really wanted.

TRACK 24: "I LOVE YOU LIKE A MADMAN"

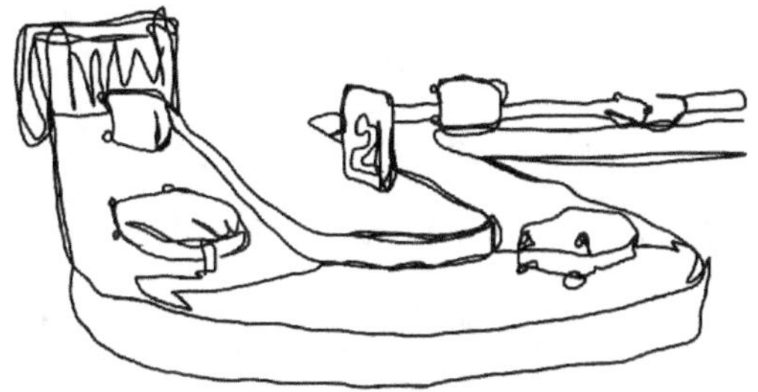

The plane is stirring restlessly. A few more reading lights flicker on as the pilot announces the aircraft's descent. I peek out the window and see a big sprawling city, wide and flat, armored with golden lights against the night.

"Hunter thinks I went to see my mom. My mom thinks I'm having a mid-life crisis."

"Why Rome?" Janet asks.

"I'm going to try and see the Pope," I say. "You know, get properly blessed, or whatever."

"Honey, I don't think you can just make an appointment with the Pope." Janet acts like she is breaking bad news.

"I know!" I say in a rush. "I don't expect to actually meet the Pope.

I am just going to attend his public Christmas blessing."

"Oh yes," she says. "I'm not Catholic by any means, but I have heard of that. Well, I think it's a brave thing you're doing. Braving the crowd, in a foreign land, to witness something so few ever get the opportunity to see."

"What are you doing in Rome?" I ask, my cheeks aflame with embarrassment upon the realization that I know nothing about her other than her name and her kindness.

"There was just space on the flight and I felt like going somewhere." She smiles and then explains. "I am a pilot."

"Oh," I say, unable to hide the surprise on my face.

"You thought women didn't fly planes?"

"No." I laugh. "I thought you were a therapist."

She laughs heartily and says, "No, no. But I do have a very good therapist myself, so maybe I have learned a few things."

We are quiet as the plane sinks through the air like it is settling at the bottom of the sea, landing on the runway.

"You know," Janet says, unbuckling her seat and stretching her neck. "I can't figure out one thing."

I look at her expectantly.

"You think you are cursed, but here you are on a plane with a plan to break that curse. Don't you see that you have faith in yourself?"

I acknowledge the spin she is putting on her words—the optimism —but my intuition tells me something bad is going to happen— something that threatens my life. I am not on a plane to break a curse. I think it is more likely that I am walking straight towards my fate, but I can't fight it anymore. It feels like destiny, not faith, and I am done running from it.

"Thank you," I say, smiling.

She smiles and pats my hand. The passengers are disembarking as we wrestle our way out of our seats. She tells me good luck. She hopes to somehow hear about what happens to me next.

I tell her I hope to fly with her in the future, and we say goodbye outside the gate. I turn my phone on. I expect a text from my mother or possibly Hunter wishing me a Happy Birthday or checking to see if I've landed in California safely.

I intend to lie.

I do not expect a text from Hunter that says, "When you land, meet me at baggage claim."

Thoughts rush past each other like rush hour traffic on a highway. *Hunter is in California. No, he is here. Impossible. He doesn't know where I've gone. How could he have gotten here before me? He is in California. But he would have spoken to my mother. She has never kept my secrets. She would tell him where I was. That means … he knows where I am, and he is here.*

I start running. I look for signs and find an image of a suitcase, despite not knowing Italian. The heat of a hundred strangers is at baggage claim, but still, I smell nicotine and rain. My eyes struggle to search the faces. My heart pounds in my throat so that I can't call out to him.

I am embraced from behind. I know it is him by the way I fit within his arms and against his chest. I vibrate at the frequency of his voice when he says my name into my ear, "Story."

I turn toward him. "What are you doing here?"

He laughs at whatever he sees on my face. "I wanted to surprise you. Happy Birthday!"

I am speechless, blindsided. Components of the equation don't add up.

"Look," he says, clutching my elbows and drawing me in, "I don't like how things ended the other night. I didn't want you to be alone on Christmas, and I didn't want to be without you. I called your mother and she told me where you were going. I hopped on the next flight." He is laughing at the confusion on my face, his smile getting more and more nervous. "Sort of a, you jump, I jump moment. If you'll have me."

"You're making a Titanic reference?" I ask him, wide-eyed. "Do you not remember that Jack dies in the end?"

Wednesday Night Playlist

TRACK 25: "BETWEEN THE DEVIL AND THE DEEP BLUE SEA"

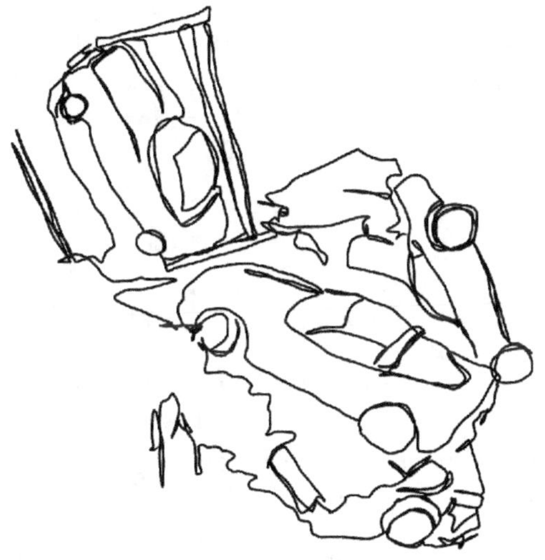

almost Valentine's Day, 2014

They keep saying we are lucky.

I'm inclined to disagree. There is a giant hole in the ground. My arms and torso are covered in scraps and cuts and rope burns. I am so tired I think I might be asleep with my eyes open. A police officer will be questioning me in a few minutes in a back room of the Corvette Museum offices. The worst part is I never got to eat my cupcake.

"I'm just blown away. This whole thing was incredible. Eight cars are missing. Eight!" A journalist says in the hallway outside.

"It's a miracle no one was hurt," the officer says.

"An honest to God miracle! Cars piled on top of each other and these two are in the one on top?"

"Is there any way these two could have done something? Planted an explosive?"

"They have the entire thing on camera. The ground just fell out from underneath them."

The officer grunts, unconvinced.

"What do you think of this headline: 'Inside the *Blue Devil,* through hell and back.' Catchy, right?" The journalist is very excited, and while I can't see the officer, I feel certain she is rolling her eyes at him.

"Finally," the officer says, and I can smell the coffee.

Hunter places the coffee in front of me. He is also covered in cuts, stone dust, and cornstarch. He kisses my cheek with a swollen lip.

The officer closes the door and the journalist sits across from us. He is wearing a button-up embroidered with a newspaper logo. The officer doesn't sit but stands and crosses her arms over her chest. She stares at us while we sip on our hot coffee.

"So," the officer says. Her eyes are sharp and she doesn't seem affected by the late hour. It is almost midnight.

"So," I say.

"Would either of you care to explain how you ended up at the bottom of a sinkhole in one of the rarest Corvettes in the world?"

We are both quiet. If I am honest, I know less than the officer knows. I stay quiet because I know Hunter is hiding something, but I don't know what.

"Wrong place, wrong time, officer," Hunter says.

She begins pacing. The journalist's eyes are glistening as if he is getting high off impossible odds. There is a good cop / bad cop thing going on, and I understand crime shows better now that I am the object of their suspicions. I don't even know what I'm protecting.

"Do you both acknowledge that museum guests are not permitted in the vehicles?"

We nod.

"Can you tell us what you were doing in the vehicle?"

We are silent. I consider telling the officer that I had been promised a cupcake in the car but I am not sure that answers her question.

"Where did the rope come from?" the officer asks.

Hunter shrugs casually.

The officer tilts her head. "Does that mean you don't know where the rope came from?"

Hunter is quietly laughing now with his hands spread in the air in surrender. "I have no clue."

The officer looks at me. "Did you bring the rope to pull yourself out of the sinkhole?"

I want to give her all the answers she seeks, but I don't have them. I only have theories that feel justified by the aforementioned sinkhole in the ground.

"I don't know where it came from, but I know why I have it," I say.

The journalist adjusts his seat and puts his pen to paper.

Hunter sighs next to me.

"I am cursed," I say.

There is a long silence. The journalist doesn't write down my words. The officer looks as though she might toss in the towel.

I clear my throat, drink my coffee, and tighten the blanket around me. I do not know what Hunter is hiding, but I know he didn't cause the sinkhole. He didn't mean for any of this to happen. Since I don't know what he is protecting, I will give my honest answer and let them think that I am crazy.

I tell them, "We tried to break the curse in Rome. I tried getting the Pope's blessing, but it didn't work."

"Do you think this is a joke?" The officer's eyes narrow on me.

"No, officer," I say.

"You really think you're cursed?" The journalist scoots his chair closer.

I nod.

"So what? You walked under a ladder and then the earth caved in beneath you?" the officer quips.

"There wasn't a ladder. It's more like I am the bad luck."

Hunter is laughing, and everyone looks toward him. He looks at me and whispers, "I don't think this is the right audience."

"What in the hell is so funny?" The officer is agitated now. People always get agitated when you talk about luck. They think there is a reason for everything, but never a god or devil with his hands in the mud.

I speak before Hunter can find the words. "Officer, did you not just call my survival a miracle? I should be dead, yes?" I lean forward despite the tremor in my voice. "You think my survival is a miraculous occurrence, but my near death must have some logical series of events? Do you think another choice would have made a difference as to where I ended up?"

The officer's eyes soften.

Hunter grabs my hand and squeezes it.

The journalist is on the edge of his seat, scribbling with his pen and paper.

"Okay," the officer says. She pulls out the empty chair across from me and sits. She leans toward me. "Okay. Please, start from the beginning."

I go to speak, but Hunter's hand squeezes again and I pause. He leans toward me.

"Let me tell the story?" He whispers like a lawyer who is trying to keep their client from looking crazy.

"Scusi?" I say. It is an inside joke we have picked up from Rome.

"Do you trust me?" He says it like Jack, with nothing to lose.

"But this is my story to tell," I say without thinking.

"Not anymore," he says, with a half smile, "This is our story now."

He's right. I realize some people have proposal stories or how-they-met stories.

Hunter and I have a survival story.

TRACK 26: "GARBAGE DAY"

Christmas Day, 2013

Hunter

Italy looked good on Fish Sticks. It was like the Italian sun filtered through air made of a different composition, and it landed on that simple country skin at the perfect angle. It was like it was right out of a movie. I might be biased though. Italy for me was new and exciting. Italy for Story was a mission and a liability.

Story started her doomsday prep questions the moment we got on a train headed into Rome.

"Did you tell your phone company you were traveling?"

I nodded.

"Does your provider work in Italy?"

I checked. Yep, it worked.

"If we get separated, we need to pick a rendezvous point. We need to get a map. We should get two maps in case we lose one."

I nodded and hid my smile.

"When is your return flight?"

I said I didn't have one.

"You're gonna get stuck here."

"When is your flight home?" I asked.

It was Friday. Friday! Story was only gonna give Italy two days. I said, "That isn't nearly long enough."

"Do you speak Italian?"

I grabbed both Story's shoulders. They were as tense as boulders on the edge of a cliff. "Calm down," I said, "It's Christmas morning. Nothing is going to happen."

Story started looking around for something wooden to knock on.

I said, "You believe in survival checklists, but I believe in the magic of Christmas."

Story's big hazel eyes stared at me, like I'd said the earth was flat. Something you have to understand is that when Story is in doomsday mode, that hazel goes more green than brown. It's a calm morning coffee with the brown eyes, and it's a bat out of hell through traffic lights with the green ones.

The way I figured it, I wasn't there to ruin Italy for her. If it was a mission Story wanted, then I'd get my boots on tight and armor up. I was exactly where I wanted to be.

"The Spanish Steps," Story decided, "the fountain at the bottom. That's our meeting point."

I had no idea what those looked like. I said, "Now, why not the

Coliseum? I know what that looks like."

Story said, "It's too big. Too much death."

"Wait," I said. "Why did we come to Rome if we weren't going to the Coliseum?"

"I came to Rome to see the Pope," Story said. "You came to Rome because you have a death wish."

"I could live with dying in Rome." I had decided that the moment I got on the plane. It felt like one of those moments. I had a choice to make, and I made it.

Story asked me to remind her to look up plane tickets to get me back home.

I didn't say I'd do nothing, 'cause I was gonna convince Story to stay a few days longer if I could. "What'd the deal with the Pope?" I asked.

Story told me, "he offers a Christmas blessing to the city and to the world. It's called Urbi et Orbi or something like that. They broadcast it all over the world."

I bit my tongue and didn't ask why we didn't just watch from home.

The train finally stopped at Roma Termini, I think it was called. I'd taken some Spanish in high school, so the signs in Italian sort of made sense to me. I was looking at some delicious Roman food, wondering if I could convince Story to stop and eat before this Pope thing.

I've never seen a person not think about food like Story. Sometimes I can put food in front of those hazel eyes, and it's gone before I can blink. But getting Story to stop and smell the gelato is the hard part.

Story had a map spread out, drawing the shortest line between the train station and the Vatican. I bet it was sixty degrees in Rome that day. It was Christmas day, and we were carrying our coats in our arms. I'm all for snow and hot cocoa, but it's something else to see Christmas with a T-shirt on. And weddings! We must have seen a dozen weddings. At one wedding, I pointed out an Alfa Romeo to

Story.

Story was too fixated on the rice being thrown over the happy couple, said, "That rice is gonna kill those birds."

My parent's neighbor back home, Barry, is a horticulturist. Well, he was at some point. He's mostly a drunk now, but he still walks around knowing everything there is to know about plants. He's the one who taught me that Bradford Pears were tree killers and Honeysuckle was an invasive species. He doesn't own a mower and lets his yard go wild. My parents hate it, but I swear I've seen more butterflies because of it. Anyways, I remember one day talking to him about birds. He said the best thing you can do for birds is to put flashy ribbon on outdoor cats. Cats are the biggest threat to birds. I asked him about all that rice married people throw. He told me that was a rumor scientists had never been able to dispel.

I told Story, "You know that's a rumor, right?" but I didn't have time to explain that no birds were in danger. The bride and groom exited the church, and rice went everywhere. It covered them, us, and the street. After the couple got to their Alfa Romeo, two doves were released into the air as the couple kissed. It was just like in the movies.

Out of nowhere, Story yelled, "Watch out!"

I ducked, 'cause that's what you do when someone yells watch out, but all I saw were two turtle doves. They went right for me, but I didn't hold it against them.

Story, on the other hand, swatted at the birds like it was a scene from a Hitchcock film.

I'm not saying I was all cool and collected, but I figured I was bigger than the birds. Besides, I sort of always thought that bird lady from Home Alone 2 was the coolest thing I'd ever seen. What I would have given for one of those birds to land on my shoulder while I just stood there.

***

"Hunter's world is right out of a fantasy cartoon, where birds dress him in the morning, and strangers high five him on the streets." I interrupted him because he was sugar coating everything. The journalist and the officer are surprised at my outburst. "Those doves were after him. He could have lost his eyes."

Hunter has his arm around me as he laughs. "I never once felt afraid of losing my eyeballs. In fact, I thought the doves were a good omen. It was a good omen for Noah."

"Isn't it also a sign of the Holy Spirit?" the journalist adds. "With John the Baptist?"

I roll my eyes.

"See!" Hunter says, gesturing to the journalist. "*Two* good signs."

"I'm not inclined to have anything with talons coming at me." The officer says it like she is on my side.

"He's acting like just because we survived, it was a good omen. That's not how it works," I say. "Cheating death never works. It'll follow you until it gets you."

The officer and the journalist hide their chuckles.

"Story never mentioned any of this in Rome, by the way. I didn't hear anything about bad luck or curses until after we saw the Pope."

"After you drilled a tiny hole into my head," I say to Hunter.

TRACK 27: "FAKE PALINDROMES"

Story

Birds aside, Rome was fine. The weather was fine. Even the wedding was kind of cool. But then the traffic got worse and the crowds got thicker. Tiny cars packed themselves into alleys, honking as if the world would fall asleep otherwise. It felt like we were making a pilgrimage across a great expanse.

Every time I turned around, Hunter was stepping into the path of a moped, or nearly getting run over as a car popped out of an alleyway. By the time we could see the dome of St. Peter's, the energy was overwhelming. Shoulders bounced off each other like we were at a rock show or a mosh-pit at Warped Tour, and we weren't even in St Peter's Square. More than 150,000 people showed up to celebrate Christmas with the new Pope Francis. A strange country is one thing. Meeting that many people in a strange country ... that'll shake anybody.

We were a block from the square when I gave up trying to fight the crowd.

Hunter had a hand to his forehead like a frontiersman scanning the horizon. "I think we can get closer," he said.

"I don't think we're really top priority here," I said, thinking about how we weren't Catholic, Italian, or Roman. We were just gringos hoping a little blessing would rub off and no one would notice.

"You are my top priority," Hunter said, elbowing me. Then, he knelt on one knee.

I'm embarrassed to say that I thought he was proposing then and there.

"Get on my shoulder," he said, motioning to his back.

The crowd began to yell, and I knew the Pope had appeared. Now was my chance. I straddled Hunter's head. I probably shouldn't have had a man's head between my legs when I saw the pope for the first time, but despite Hunter's best efforts, we never even got close to the Pope. The man was never more than a tiny dot against a red backdrop. Hoisted on Hunter's shoulders, my feet and knees brushed the shoulders of those around us. I couldn't have found space to stand on the ground even if I'd wanted to.

When I heard the Pope begin to speak, it was just an echo. It was soft and kind, slow and methodical. I absorbed the consonants and vowels that rolled off his tongue. I confessed my sins in return.

I did not feel some magical weight lifted. There was no vision in the sky. There was only the magnetic energy of thousands and thousands of people soaking in the calmness of the tiny white dot against the red background—souls grasping at eternal peace and forgiveness of their sins.

He didn't speak for long. As soon as a tangible tranquility settled over the sea of souls, it erupted in applause. Banners flew high, and fingers outstretched towards the white dot. Before I could ask myself if the blessing had worked or if it had been enough, we were moving. The crowd shifted like an avalanche, like a mountainside coming apart in multiple directions at once.

It is not fun to be on the shoulders of someone, who has no control over what direction they are being pushed. I tried to stabilize myself with my hands on Hunter's shoulders but I eventually had to wrap one arm around his head and one around his neck. I was surely choking him as he made his best effort at heading towards the edge of the crowd and to the nearest building where I could see the alcove he was aiming for.

I loosened the grip of my arms but tightened my legs around his torso. It was like I was playing gladiator at the city pool on my dad's shoulders. My dad would hold me as I tried to push my cousins off the shoulders of their dads. I was pretty competitive as a child, and the rule was that as long as you weren't knocked off, you didn't lose. I would just never let go of my dad. He got to a point that he wouldn't do it anymore. He said I had too much fun drowning him.

We very nearly made it to the alcove, where there would have been enough room for us to crouch, but I wasn't paying attention and neither was Hunter. My head smacked into the horizontal beam across the top. I fell back and took him down with me.

TRACK 28: "I'LL BELIEVE IN ANYTHING"

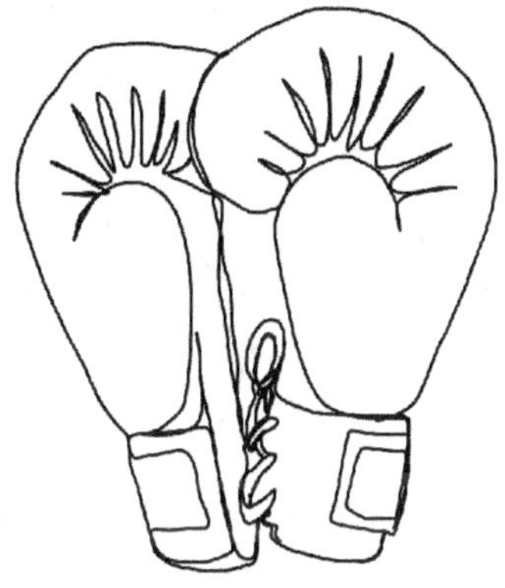

Hunter

That was my bad. I didn't think about how Goliath we were together. I plowed Story right into that stone support. It didn't hurt me too badly. Story's legs were wrapped around me, so I fell back onto some cushioning. I can't believe we weren't knocked out. I was the first to move. I rolled over to check on Story, and some older woman passing by got the wrong impression. She wasn't about to walk away either. I tried to straighten up and look decent, but my back got stuck. The muscles locked so tightly that I was stuck there with my face to Story's crotch right there in the Vatican.

The woman moved to stand over us, muttering something in Italian. She flagged down a gentleman, who looked at me like he might wring my neck.

"Scusi," the man said. He said more Italian, but Story sat up and just threw a thumbs up.

I said, "Story, tell the man, I'm not a rapist."

Story started miming our gladiator accident: finger puppets falling to their demise.

That man looked more confused than if we had kept speaking a foreign language.

"Está bien," I managed to say, even though I knew it wasn't Italian.

He asked us in broken english if we needed an ambulance.

Story pointed at me and used made up hand signals to tell him my back was hurt. She finally asked the man, "Help me lift him?"

The man helped Story, and then me, get to the wall. We just sat there like bums.

The man asked us again if we needed an ambulance.

We gave him two thumbs up and he seemed satisfied. He corralled the old woman away with him.

All of a sudden, Story was crying like a faucet and mumbling about how something didn't work.

"What didn't work?" I asked. I didn't understand. I was focused on the muscles in my back, and the crowd was still loud outside the alcove. Eventually, I managed to put two and two together. Story thought something was gonna happen after the Pope's blessing.

"What did you think would happen, exactly?" I asked.

Story looked broken. I hated it. I hated that the truth was about to come out. It's like when someone's secrets and inner-workings are what you love about them, and at a certain point, when their defenses are worn down, you just want to help them build them back up and shield your eyes so the spell isn't broken, you know?

Story thought if we could be blessed by the Pope, then all the bad things would stop happening, even just for a day or an afternoon, but it hadn't worked. We were doomed.

I inched myself around to face those big, wet hazel eyes. I said, "Gravity doesn't discriminate. That's one rule not even the Pope can fight."

Story didn't think I was funny.

I said, "This wasn't a tragedy. Us falling was just … life."

Story is normally quiet, but words flow from me like salmon swimming up river, fighting the current. They come all at once. Irreverent. Spray and pray. If a couple don't get through, I'll try again.

Story's words don't work like that. They have been carefully weighed, stacked, and cemented into place. Then, they're prayed on and blessed. Then, they're put to the test and usually put to death. If they escape, it's because they've survived everything thrown at them. I had forgotten that. I had tried to argue that everything was fine as if my words could out number Story's.

So, I let Story cry. It hurt like hell to think I couldn't do anything to help. I just kept thinking that there ain't no shame in feeling what you feel. Why do we always try to stop the bad feelings?

Story started laughing out of nowhere, and asked me, "Do you believe in the Devil?"

I nodded.

"Do you think he makes deals with people?"

I thought of gold fiddles in Georgia and nodded.

"Well, I think the devil hangs around airports, looking for runaways with daddy issues."

I stared for a long time. Something about the image that popped up in my head sounded familiar. "Wait!" I shook my head. "You think Mr. Fox is the Devil? Like *the* Devil. Not just some creepy old man who bought you a drink? Devil with a capital D?"

Story nodded with eyes hulkishly green.

"That is crazy," I said. Then it clicked. That was why we'd come all this way. Story thought the Pope would rectify some mistake made over a year ago. Story thought every bad thing that had happened was because the Devil granted an unhappy wife the freedom to walk away.

"It's not a bad crazy," I said. "It's like, when you told me about rice killing birds, and I told you that's not what happens. It's *crazy* how an entire nation can get an idea in their head and not know how far off they are. It's like that. You've just got it in your head that he was the Devil but he was just, like, an old man who crossed a boundary and imposed his advice on you."

Story whispered so low I had to lean in to hear the truth. "But it's not just what he said. I've had visions of a disaster, like an earth-shattering disaster. It feels so real—"

I whispered back, "Is this like a premonition?"

Story nodded.

I thought, *Well hell. Who am I to decide what's crazy or not.* There I was on my ass, thinking life was random and chaotic. I'd always been a roll-with-the-punches kind of guy, but there Story was, trying to argue that everything had a reason. Life was filled with purpose and intention. Instead of dodging the punches, we could try to appeal to the person in the gloves. Story wasn't satisfied with Elvis Presley handing out a shitty future. Story was gonna waltz behind the curtain and speak to whoever was in charge.

I told Story I believed everything. I said, "Let me help. If the Pope didn't fix it, maybe we go to Pan."

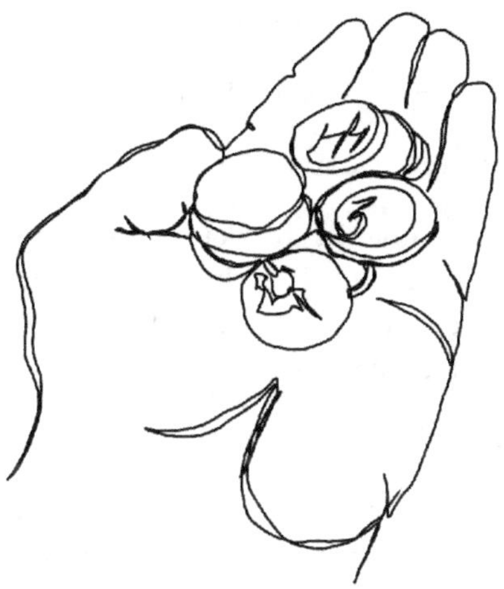

Story

Pan was closed on Christmas Day. Hunter and I had to wait until the next day. Instead, we succumbed to jet lag. We slept for twelve hours under the protection of the four chubby cherubs suspended from each post of a wrought iron bed frame.

We woke up to the smell of brioches. When we emerged from the hotel room, we set out into the buildings painted like stony pastries, pastel-colored in the morning light, and dodged mopeds as they outran the taxis. We learned to ignore crosswalk signs. We crossed when someone speaking Italian crossed.

Where the paths opened up, cars circled us like sharks. Signs for Gelato greeted us with a hospitable wave. Then, we'd squeeze back into the narrow paths between the main Via Dels and Piazza Del's, like the muscles of an esophagus carries food from the mouth to the stomach, the center. When the pavement turned to cobblestone, I could feel the rumble of the city beneath my feet. The one thing about Rome I discovered right away was that its labyrinthine streets kept everything just around the corner. It held endless slight lefts and slight rights, as if right angles would give away its secrets too easily. Finally, we were squeezed out at the entrance to the Pantheon.

Tourists and tour guides spouted facts like *113 AD* and *142 ft* and *largest unreinforced concrete dome in the world.*

"What do we do now?" I asked Hunter.

"We pray to Pan for a cleansing. A rain."

We stood directly beneath the oculus and prayed to Pan, which is to say we prayed to all the gods. When that didn't immediately work, we prayed to the state of Italy. When that didn't work, I feared we had prayed to nothing but a weatherman.

"Got another idea?" I asked.

He asked me to get the map as he pulled me back to the plaza outside the pantheon. When I unfolded the map, he said, "The Trevi Fountain!" Hunter shoved his hand in his pocket and pulled out his American change, "Do you think we have to exchange our currency to make a wish? Do you think that counts against us?"

Just in case, we exchanged our coins at a kiosk on the way to the fountain. We could only get close to the water on the far-right side by the statue of Health feeding her sacred serpent.

Hunter had the coins in his pocket. He was armed to wish our wishes, but I was looking at the pool. The water was a blue like the portrait of an iceberg. It had peaks and valleys with translucent layers that both shut you out and drew you in—Cerulean, Sapphire, Aegean, and Arctic, the color of Jack's skin as he sank into the ocean bed.

I was about to run to grab Hunter's hand and go anywhere else when we were accosted by a woman with jet black hair and eyes like coal.

"Making a wish?" She said with her large eyes on me. She smelled like Lily of the Valley.

"Yep," Hunter said, smiling and leaning towards the woman. "Did you make your wish already?"

She said, "No, dear, I am happy as a pea in a pod." She grabbed my hand. "But this one. This one you have to worry about."

"Scusi?" I asked. My heart was going a mile a minute.

She shook my arm and indicated the naked ring finger of my left hand. She said I must be looking for a husband. The smile on her face looked like a caricature on the back of a cereal box.

She turned her smile to Hunter, "If you won't do it, someone else will." She looked back at me, and suddenly, I felt the cold metal of a coin against my palm. "One says you'll return to Rome." She placed another coin in my palm. "Throw two and find love." With the third coin, she pulled me in and whispered, "Toss three coins and you will be married soon."

She winked at me as I recoiled from her. The three coins were heavy on the lines of my palm.

"That's a bit rude," Hunter said out of nowhere. "I think we can decide for ourselves what we wish for." He shifted his stance, grabbed the three coins from my hand, and gave them back to the woman. "Thank you for your unsolicited opinion."

The woman smiled, slightly more obtuse. She visibly straightened her spine, but still wasn't quite as tall as me. "You are absolutely right, young man. Life is too short to get in a rush."

Then she winked and left us, vanishing into the thick body of people biding their time to get a good spot by the fountain.

"That was rude," I told him.

"Tell me about it."

"No, you were rude!" I clarified.

"Me?"

"We could have just said *Okay, thank you. Happy New Year*."

"Oh, did you want to throw a stranger's coins under the pretense of getting married. My bad, I thought we came here to break a curse."

"She didn't need to know what we *actually* wished."

Hunter looked at me with big pitiful eyes. He said, "We don't have to pretend to take her advice. There's nothing rude about being honest."

But that was the wrong thing to tell me. I was still a little jaded. I knew what he said was reasonable, but all I kept thinking about was Hunter refusing to marry me. I said, "I'm so forgetful. I almost forgot how much marriage is off the table. I'm so glad I didn't waste that poor woman's coins or her good intentions."

Hunter's hand was open. His palm was up and filled with the coins from his pockets. He started to speak, but I didn't want to hear it. I grabbed everything in his hand.

"Don't bother," I yelled. I threw every bit of it into the fountain. It scattered across the surface clear to the other side. "There. I wish I could be put out of my misery." I stalked off without thinking about how the universe would choose to put me out of my misery.

***

Hunter isn't looking at me. There is a smile trying to break out on his face. I can tell by the way he spins his coffee cup on the table that he is nervous, like he is about to confess something.

"Well," he says, shaking his head, "I must say, this is not at all how I thought this would go down. If you can allow me a moment to think about my words …" He pats his pocket. "Can I smoke in here?"

"No," the officer says without hesitation.

He nods and orients his knees towards me. "Okay, I'm just going to say it."

He doesn't say anything right away. I can hear the groan of two chairs across the table as the journalist and the officer lean in closer. I can hear warm air through vents. I can hear mechanical beeps of machinery on the other side of the Corvette museum. I am losing patience.

"Story, there was a ring in my hand, with the coins …" He coughs and gestures with his hands, reenacting my actions. "… the coins you threw in the fountain."

I stare at Hunter's empty hand, frozen, tangled up in blue. I am Jack, sinking into an unforgiving dark, blue ocean.

TRACK 30: "PURITAN HEART"

Hunter

I wasn't gonna give up that quickly. When Story stormed off, I took off my boots, socks, and coat. I rolled up the hem of my pants and shirt as far as I could.

"Don't do it," a man said to me under his breath, knowing what I was about to do. He was with a woman who I assumed was his wife.

"I have to get something back," I said. It was at least fifty degrees outside, so I didn't think it'd be that bad, but when I stepped in, the water was like little pins and needles.

"You will be arrested," the man said.

"You will get sick," the woman said.

"Well, I can't afford another, so..." I stepped both feet into the water. It reached almost to the top of my thighs. It was torture.

"It is a heavy fine," the man said. "At least five hundred euro." The man was no longer whispering as he watched over his shoulders.

I laughed as I stepped toward the center of the fountain. "I'm between a rock and a hard place. I hope they will have pity on me."

"Officers are coming," he said, pointing toward the staircase down to the fountain. They were yelling in English, "Get out of the fountain!" That tells you how many dumb Americans try to go for an illegal swim.

"What are you looking for?" the woman asked.

I told them it was an engagement ring.

The woman reverted to a language I didn't know and pulled on the man's sleeves. He argued with her for a minute or two and then ripped off his boots and joined me.

"What are you doing?" I asked him.

"My wife says if I love her, I will help you."

"What about the officers? The fine?" my toes were numb at this point.

"She says if I love her, I will pay."

"So, I guess you love her."

"No, she is dreadful," he said, looking down into the water. "I am here to find the ring first and save you from a similar dreadful fate."

He wasn't joking.

When he noticed me staring at him, he said, "The universe tried to tell you not to do it, and you are stubborn. If I find the ring, I'll toss it among the pickpockets, and you will be saved. If you find the ring, I will pay the fine and you will get married."

I told him he was crazy.

He just nodded and looked back into the water, searching for the engagement ring.

The heat was on now. Suddenly the water was *too clear*. I was picking up everything that didn't look like a coin. I kept one eye on the fountain floor and one on him. I searched with an imaginary grid, so that I wouldn't miss a spot but he let the wind blow him wherever, like the universe would lead him straight to Story's ring. I was getting real nervous. The officers were yelling at us. Tourists were videoing us.

Then, I heard him. "Ah ha!" He said, holding the ring high. I saw that stone in his hand and I knew he had found it. You can bet your last dollar I tackled him. We both fell into the water, fully immersed in the freezing cold. I could see the ring in his hand, but by this point, my hands were so numb I couldn't grip anything. My fingers fumbled with his. I bet we dropped it back into the fountain a half-dozen times.

Finally though, I managed to get it. I clenched it in my fist so tight it cut my palm. I practically ran on top of the water back to the police officers. They were so angry, they never let me speak. They pulled me away by my elbows. They wouldn't even let me get my shoes or coat. I can't remember what they said. All I could do was clench the ring in my hand. I was just a dumb American, finally with something to lose.

The man eventually joined me. His wife carried my clothes and yelled at him the whole time. When they handed us both our fines, he walked directly to an ATM and paid the officers.

The man shook my hand and said, "You will propose now?"

"Yes," I said, "if nothing else goes wrong."

"You will need a good bottle of wine and good cheese," he said.

His wife said, "She is lucky to have you."

I didn't have the heart to tell them that I wasn't so sure about that.

TRACK 31: "LET'S KEEP IT THAT WAY"

Story

It was the golden hour when he found me on the Spanish steps. He carried a paper bag in his arm. He pulled out a bottle of cabernet, gouda, a soft cheese I didn't recognize, prosciutto, salami, olives, and ciabatta bread. He had no plates, glasses, or utensils, and he was in new clothes.

He knelt on the step below me. I watched him reach into his pocket like he was about to pull out a ring. I thought, no, he must be getting a bottle opener. I couldn't take it. I blurted out, "Please sit next to me. It looks like you're about to propose."

He froze and looked at me sideways. He said, "What if I was about to propose?"

"You were gonna lay all this food out and not let me eat it?" I asked.

"I thought you'd be more excited about my undying love for you," he said.

"No," I said.

"Okay." Hunter laughed. "Eat first, and then we'll discuss our soulmate-ship."

I started on the olives. He sat next to me and twisted off the cap to the wine. From our vantage point on the steps, we could see most of the sky as the sun sank beneath the tops of the buildings. The clouds were painted in purple and gold. Starlings flew back and forth in great black shrinking shapes.

"What are we doing for New Year's this year?" Hunter asked, handing me cheese and meat.

I shrugged and said, "I'll be home, and you'll be stuck in Rome."

Hunter suddenly remembered I was supposed to fly out the next day. He asked me if I'd consider staying.

I told him, "That's a really sweet notion, but I think I'm ready to be home."

The birds were thickening in the air. Their silhouettes went from shadowless black to iridescent reflections of the glow of the sinking sun. They shifted from red to orange to yellow, and then as if flipping a switch, they turned from purple to blue while they performed their synchronized dance in the sky. *Murmuration*. That's what it was called. I remembered a nature show on TV I had watched with my dad.

"Reminds me of a Windows screensaver," Hunter said, watching the birds with me.

"It's how they evade predator birds like hawks or falcons, by hypnosis and confusion."

"I don't get how they change directions so quickly. Do you think they can read each other's minds?" Hunter asked me.

I told him, "My dad always said it was just like racing cars or dirt bikes. Take care of the front of your car and let everyone behind you take care of the back of your car."

"That's like playing music too," Hunter said, "If everyone's paying attention, you can change direction any time you want. If you look too far ahead or try to predict where it will go, you'll miss what's happening in the moment."

The flap of a hundred thousand wings reverberated around us. Hunter leaned back on his elbow with prosciutto rolled in his fingers. A busker played saxophone at the bottom of the Spanish steps. Mozzarella melted in my mouth.

The starlings pulsed like a beating heart in the sky.

For a blissful second, I was thinking neither in the future nor the past, not regretting or dreading. I was salty meat, a thousand wings, cool December air, and sweet wine. My pulse was the vibrations of ancient footsteps on stone. I was a shapeshifter that was impervious to a predator.

Boom!

I didn't think. I just acted. I launched myself over Hunter.

Boom!

With my back to Rome, I felt the soft patter of something scatter and splat on the ground around us.

Boom!

Hunter was laughing beneath the weight of me.

"I thought it was a gunshot!" I said. The people and steps around us were spotted like a dalmatian.

Hunter pointed out white starbursts in the sky. "Fireworks must have scared the birds."

"That's ..." I looked at the ruined food on the Spanish Steps. "That's bird shit, isn't it?"

When we both got to our feet, Hunter asked me if I had been

protecting him.

I repeated, "I thought it was gunshots!"

He laughed at me and said, "Well, if protecting me from a rain of bird poop isn't love, I don't know what is." He used his coat sleeve to try to wipe away the spots on my back.

When we had done the best we could, we saw that instead of spots we wore smears of white and gray. We were walking abstract paintings. There was no hope. We tossed the food but kept the wine.

Drinking straight from the bottle, Hunter said, "At least one of our prayers was answered. We asked for rain, didn't we?"

TRACK 32: "THIS YEAR"

Hunter

I meant to propose to Story the next morning. I was going to sneak out before Story woke up. I would find a Christmas market still open. I thought I'd get mulled wine and cider with waffles and chocolates. I had even picked out a place to buy fresh flowers. I thought it would all fall into place.

At about three in the morning, I got sick. I'd never been so sick in my life. I had diarrhea first. Then, I was vomiting. Suddenly, I didn't know what *end* to expect *what* to come out. I moved to the bathtub where I ran the water and desperately tried to clean up after myself with nothing but hotel shampoo and bar soap.

Story knocked on the door, and I pleaded for us to stay on

opposite sides of the door.

"I think I have food poisoning," I said, still on my hands and knees.

"From meat and cheese?" Story said it like it was impossible.

I said, "Maybe it was bad cheese."

The overhead light came on, and I could see the shape of Story's wringing hands through the translucent shower curtain.

"It might be salmonella from the bird poop," Story guessed, which I thought was even more preposterous.

"Like raw eggs in cookie dough?" I asked while butt naked and squeezing shampoo out around me just to mask any lingering smell.

Story explained, "It's bird shit on raw eggs that gives you Salmonella."

I laid there with my eyes closed until I thought it had all passed. I dreamed of birds making cookies and letting me lick the spoon. I jerked awake to see Story kneeling over me. The shower was turned off, and a clean towel was being offered to me.

"Can I die from salmonella?" I asked as I sat up.

Story laughed at me. "I don't know. How about we try to find a doctor?"

"No," I said. "I don't want to go to a doctor."

Story tried to tell me it would be in my best interest, but see, I don't like doctors. I let Story not like weatherman and believe in superstitions. I only asked for this one unreasonable thing.

I'm not proud to say it, but I wanted to call my dad.

Story found my phone and my dad's number and put him on speakerphone.

"Hey Buddy!" My dad's overly optimistic voice rang through the hotel bathroom. He asked me about Rome.

I said, "Rome is great. The Pope was great. Can you do me a favor?

Can you connect me with Jeff and not tell mom?"

My dad was quiet. I could hear him walk through the house and out the back door. I recognized the squeal of the screen door's hinges as he said, "You've put me in a tough spot, son. You know your mom's still pretty mad. What exactly is wrong?"

I told him that we thought it was food poisoning and possibly Salmonella. I told him I just wanted an English opinion on my symptoms.

My dad said he'd get Jeff to call me back. He hung up, and the first question out of Story's mouth was, "What is your mom mad about?"

"Nothing," I said. "Don't worry about it."

Story had the nerve to tell me, "Please don't lie."

That was a pot callin' the kettle black. Story lied about going to California, but I couldn't conceal information that wasn't relevant?

But Story looked pretty pitiful and told me, "Consider what it feels like when not even my own mother keeps my secrets. Mother would rather betray me and give you the information you want."

I hadn't thought of it that way, but this was different. I was trying to protect all parties involved. Story wasn't mad about me not talking about my mom. I knew what the real problem was and I was about to say it when my phone rang.

It was Jeff. He said, I should got to the doctor, but if I was gonna be stubborn, he also thought it sounded like Salmanella or food poisoning. He said both would pass in a few days, if my symptoms didn't get worse. He told me to hunker down for a few days though. Said the first 24 hours would be the worst.

I didn't even make it through the phone call with Jeff before I dry heaved into the toilet.

It was well into the evening when I realized Story hadn't flown back home and left me. In fact, Story spent the next couple days hiding out with me in a cramped Italian hotel room bathroom. We piled blankets on the floor the first day. I was able to move to the bed the second day. Story kept me stocked with water and crackers while I watched the clouds cross the sky through the window.

By the third day, I was feeling better. I walked myself to the bathroom without help and ate all of my breakfast and most of Story's.

Just when I was feeling like walking around Rome some more, I noticed something was wrong. Story's eyes were pretty darn green.

While I was puking out my guts, Story had been keeping an eye on flights. Turns out everything was either booked full, or ungodly expensive. I found myself in another predicament. I thought I had an answer. I thought I could kill two birds with one stone or catch two butterflies with one net. I went to the bathroom and called my mom.

My mom answered immediately and asked me, "Are you okay?"

"Yeah," I said, with a laugh. "I'm great."

"Your father already told me." She said, "Did you really think he could keep a secret? He lasted ten seconds thinking he was sneaking around talking to Jeff. You think I can't get Jeff to tell me when my firstborn son is sick?"

Well, at least I tried, you know? I told my mom I felt much better than I did.

"Good enough to fly home?" she asked.

I told her Story was having trouble finding a flight we could afford.

My mother said, "Well, Story doesn't know what this mother is capable of. If you're ready to come home, I'll get you home. Mark my word, you'll be here before the end of the year."

The end of the year was in two days.

"I bet you regret missing Christmas now, don't you?" she said.

"I regret the salmonella," I said, truthfully. "I will take warnings about bird poop and raw eggs seriously from here on out."

"I want a redo for Christmas," she said. "I'll take care of everything to get you home—to get you both home. I'll take care of the trains, planes, and hotels. I'll find some men with boats if I have to, but

I want a Christmas redo."

I had sort of seen this coming. My mother would make something happen if that was what she wanted, and if the good Lord willed it. She also knew I was gonna do what I was gonna do, 'cause this apple didn't fall far from the tree.

"Alright, Mom. We'll do Christmas again when we get back," I promised her.

I told her I loved her, hung up, and hobbled to the door. When I opened it, Story fell into the floor.

"Scusi?" I said. I was met with silence. I asked point blank, "Were you eavesdropping?"

Story rose and snatched my phone from my hands.

I tried to wrestle for it. I didn't even know what I was wrestling for, I just knew something was about to go awry. I was still pretty weak, and Story slipped right out of my hands. Credit, where credit is due, Story's stronger than me on most of my good days.

Story's voice saying my mother's name had an effect on me like a tornado siren. Nothing could be done but to run and find cover.

Story paced the hotel room, smiling and making deals with my mother, which was more dangerous than the Devil himself. By the time they were done plotting and scheming, we were on our way to Belgium.

TRACK 33: "WHEN I PAINT MY MASTERPIECE"

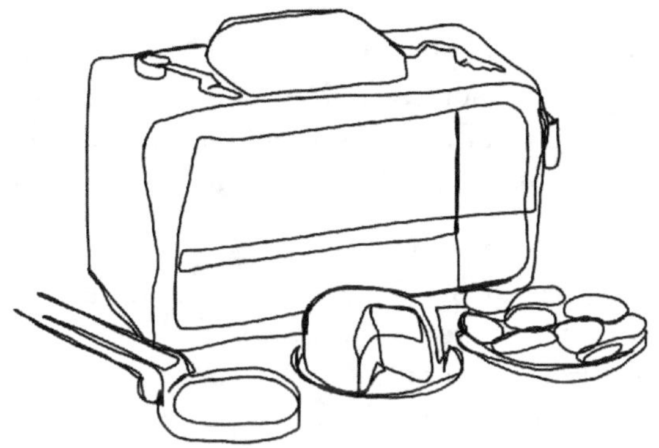

Story

Susan had seen something on the television about the Christmas Market in Brussels, and I promised her that we'd find her a special ornament for Christmas 2.0.

"I didn't realize we were that close to Belgium," Hunter said to me on a train on our way to catch a bus.

"We're twenty-four hours away," I said.

"A day?" He nearly fell out of his seat. "A full day?"

I pleaded with him. "Please don't tell your mother. It's worth it. Whatever she wants and wherever she wants it from is worth it. The flight out of Brussels alone was premium tickets because that's all that was left."

"A day," he repeated, half delirious.

"Are you sure you're feeling okay?" I asked him, putting my hand to his forehead. "You're beginning to repeat yourself."

The long ride didn't bother me. I was dreaming of Swiss mountains and snow, or maybe Paris or Austria. I had no idea what path the bus would take. I just thought I would get to see more of Europe.

But the first bus barely got us to North Italy. We didn't board the next bus until 4 pm. The sun set an hour later. Switzerland was a pitch-black landscape. With nothing to see outside, we turned our attention inside to a group of passengers that had started a card game.

Hunter and I watched, with our knees in our seats and our elbows hanging over our headrests. I never caught the name of the game. Among the six playing, they would all reveal a card simultaneously. Whoever's cards matched would start screaming animal noises at each other. After a while, we realized that certain animals had been assigned to everyone. If you called out someone's animal noise three times first, you won all their cards. That was how you won the game.

The best part was realizing that the noise a rooster makes is not universal. In English we say *cockadoodledoo*. But in French, it's more like *cocorico*. In Italian, it's *chicchirichi*. A dog can go *woof woof, bau bau, ouah ouah*.

Eventually, Hunter and I joined in. We grabbed a piece of paper from a cup. Hunter got a pig, and I got a fox. I proceeded to flip my cards, still leaning over my seat. Hunter oinked at a man who took his cards and purred at a woman who gave him her cards. When one of my cards matched someone else's, the entire back half of the bus broke into the song, "What does the fox say?"

Everybody burst into laughter. I laughed until I peed myself, which caused Hunter to laugh until he threw up. We were quarantined in the front of the bus, wrapped in blankets and supplied with throw-up bags. We fell asleep sometime after midnight, somewhere in the Swiss Alps. The three stars of Orion's belt looked back at me like three wisemen returning home.

We woke up in Brussels. We stared at a new map, in a new language, through a new city, decorated like Christmas, as if it wasn't about to be 2014. We walked around like we were on eggshells. We ate mussels cautiously and drank mulled wine with reverence. We stuffed our bags with waffles and chocolates. We found ornaments for Hunter's Mom. I found one for my mom too. After only a few hours in Brussels, we started to believe everything would be okay.

When we boarded our plane at noon, Hunter's mom was waking up in Kentucky. When we landed at our first layover in Moscow, it was after sundown. On our second flight, we lost track of the time and the time zone. Somewhere over the Atlantic, we decided we'd pick our own new beginning of the year.

I got souvenir treats from our bags. We sandwiched chocolate between waffles, and Hunter started laughing. I asked him what was so funny.

"A couple years back," he said, "Simon ruined a good cast iron skillet trying to make a pancake omelet with chocolate. He had this big plan for breakfast in bed for Mother's Day. He didn't want any help of course."

"Susan must have been furious," I said.

Hunter shrugged, still laughing. "She definitely had a small, quiet funeral for the skillet, but she still has it. She keeps it around to remember how sweet Simon can be."

I asked Hunter, "Did you ever have an Easy Bake Oven?"

Hunter shook his head no.

I told him it was essentially a tart warmer. "It was a toy with a light bulb that warmed special recipes of food. My household was too poor to afford these prepackaged recipes so I would cook whatever I could steal from the kitchen, the floor, or the yard." Hunter winced, already knowing where this was going. I said, "I'd make cupcakes, except they'd never fully cook because it was only a lightbulb. My mom and dad did their best to pretend to be excited when I handed out my inedible abominations. After I left a few in my dad's Corvette for him, I was banned from cooking and from food in the Corvette in one fatal swoop."

We had run out of chocolate and waffles. We were using every last inch of our tiny napkins to wipe our hands when Hunter asked me, "What's wrong with the Corvette anyways?"

"Possibly nothing," I said. "When I was twelve, he wrecked it. He said he wasn't drunk, but it was hard to believe a sober person could have survived. He broke a rib and his right orbital socket. He still had an eyepatch when my mom gave him an ultimatum. She told him if he wanted to live to see me grow up, he was going to have to make a choice. I think she meant for him to stop drinking, but he decided to park the Corvette and repair it a little bit at a time. I used to help him. I mean as much as a kid can actually help. I'm sure it was just a way for him to keep it. When my mom would say he needed to get rid of it, he'd call her heartless for taking away the one thing we could do together."

Hunter mulled over my words. When a flight attendant passed by, he flagged him down and got us a few of those tiny bottles of wine.

We toasted to the new year.

"To breaking curses," I said.

We landed in New York before 10 pm—two hours before midnight —like the universe just wouldn't let the year die.

***

"Why didn't you propose then?" The journalist interrupts me to ask Hunter.

Hunter shifts in his seat. I can see his fingers itching for a cigarette. "Everything was going so well." He laughs. "I didn't want to mess it up."

"Is that what you were doing in the car?" the officer asks abruptly. "Proposing?"

Hunter grabs my hand and looks from me to the officer. "We were only supposed to be in the car for a couple minutes. I didn't think anyone would even notice. I thought it was either a good idea or a good story."

"Looks like you got a good story," the journalist says. His eyes are wide with humor.

"Where's the ring?" the officer asks, not missing a beat.

Hunter picks up my hand and kisses it. He takes a big breath and says, "I don't know." He looks so incredibly sad.

"You lost it in the sink hole?"

Hunter shakes his head, staring at my finger. "No. I thought I brought it into the museum with me. I stuffed it into a cupcake before we got here, but when I went to get the cupcake from my bag, it wasn't there."

"You forgot it at home?" The journalist asks.

Hunter finally releases my hand. "I think Story handed it off to a good Samaritan in a Walmart parking lot."

TRACK 34: "LONG WAY HOME"

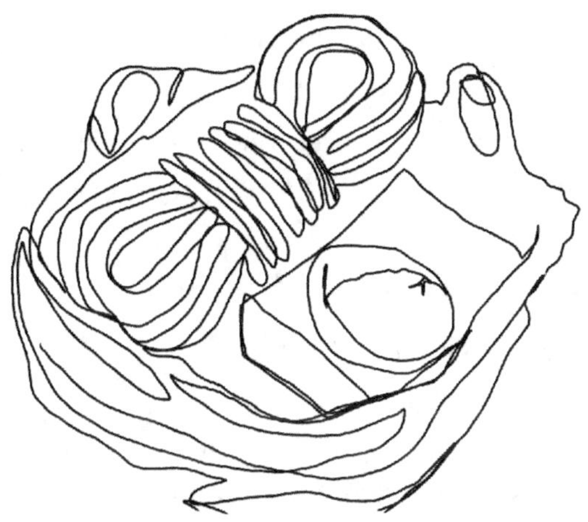

Hunter

I lied to Story. I said I was driving across the state to buy a guitar. I fluttered my eyelashes and really stressed how much I wanted the company. At first, I thought I was going to have to beg. Normally, Story is game for a trip. I drive a little hatchback with a manual transmission, and it's fun to drive. Back home, though, the roads were dusted in snow. Story thought it would be better to wait a few days. I should have just waited. I should have listened. Instead, I claimed the guitar was too good a deal. Someone else would snatch it up.

I had it all worked out. On the way here, I stopped at a Walmart under the pretense that I needed a money order. I thought I'd be able to sneak in and sneak out, but Story insisted on coming with me. We walked in together. As soon as Story disappeared into the restroom, I snuck off to the bakery and picked out a cupcake. Then, I ran to where they put bouquets together.

I asked the florist, "Could you just throw something together?"

The florist looked at me with her head to one side. "Throw something together?" Her eyes widened. "You think that's what I do? Throw things in a box? Toss them in the air and they fall into a vase like this?" She pointed towards the arrangements in the cooler between us.

I apologized and started again. "I just meant to say, it doesn't have to require a lot of effort. I just want the flowers to conceal the ring."

"So, it can be ugly?" She returned to the arrangement she was working on, snipping the ends of roses like she was wishing they were attached to me.

"No," I said, "Make it look good, just—"

She cut me off. "Just throw them together?"

There I was standing like an idiot, looking over my shoulder like I was trying to rob the place. I gave up and pleaded with her. "I want you to use your skill and whatever effort you deem appropriate to cover this tiny cupcake in flowers so that they can tastefully conceal this humble ring that has damn near made it around the world." I put on my best smile. "I'm going to propose today!"

I could tell she didn't care and didn't want to do it, but she finally reached out for the cupcake. I'd say she worked quickly, but I'm sure she was just ready to get rid of me. She started to show me the cupcake, but I told her I wanted it to be a surprise. She boxed it up. I couldn't even tell you what it looked like. I ran straight to the parking lot and saw Story under the hood of my car.

I had left the lights on.

Story asked me if I had any jumper cables.

"We can push start it," I said, hoping all this would distract Story from the bag swinging in my hand.

Story was making a strong argument for taking the battery inside to the auto department to see if they could charge it, but I was looking at the time and thinking there was no way we'd make it to the museum before it closed. I panicked and took the first opportunity that walked up.

A younger guy walked past the car. He looked like a kid or maybe a teenager. He carried a single plastic bag, just like me. I asked him if he'd help push start our car. He didn't even hesitate.

Story took both of our bags and hopped in the passenger seat. I steered as we pushed the car out of the parking spot and down the aisle. I was on the driver side, and the stranger was on Story's side. When it got going, I hopped in the driver's seat and popped the clutch.

Then, I'm guessing, Story handed my bag right out the window to that young man.

I completely abandoned the guitar lie. We were so late I thought my whole plan was a wash. When I pulled into the museum parking lot twenty minutes before they closed, Story was confused six ways to Sunday. I decided I'd just tell the truth, that I'd got her a cupcake, which would only ruin part of the surprise. We barely made it in time to convince the staff at the entrance to let us in. Story was smiling so big when we walked into the dome that it was all worth it—right there.

Story set her eyes on the blue one—the *blue devil*.

I was the first to step over the barrier separating us from the cars.

"Are we really going to do this?" Story asked, laughing but also following me over the barrier.

"We're gonna eat the cupcake in the car." I pointed to the blue devil. "This bajillion dollar car."

There wasn't another soul in there with us. The doors were unlocked, so we flung them open and slipped inside.

Story pulled the Walmart bag out right away. I was trying to find my words. I said, "Story, I'm sorry this has all been a big mess. Actually, I'm not sorry. I'm not gonna apologize for nothing. I take credit and pride in everything we've ever done or not done. I think we've arrived exactly where we are supposed to be."

Like I said, I couldn't find my words. I was just spoutin' off my thoughts, like maybe one of them would stick. I watched Story's fingers untie the knot in the handles of the Walmart bag and rummage inside it, waiting until the cupcake emerged.

"Are we blowing up a cake?" Story pulled a box of cornstarch out of the bag.

I looked at that box of cornstarch so hard. I thought that disgruntled Walmart Florist had stolen my cupcake and my ring. I thought that was an unfair punishment for my crime of offending her. When I reached into the bag again, a bundle of rope came out. No label, no tag, nothing. Just a bundle of rope, neatly wrapped like a cylinder.

I had cornstarch in one hand and rope in the other when I heard a hollow noise. I looked around the skydome. Nothing seemed wrong, but Story looked at me like a momma possum with a dozen babies hanging on for dear life. The lights flickered off and on. The Corvette bucked.

The car next to us dropped through the floor, then the one beside it. Their rubber tires clawed at the edges like wild animals. The overhead lights in the skydome flashed across the glossy paint. I went to open the car door to get out. I don't know if I was running or getting out to get a better look. I know I registered what I saw. I just don't know if I was making a conscious decision about it.

That's when Story put a hand on mine and without saying a word, I knew to stay put.

***

Story

Everyone is quiet when Hunter finishes.

If I focus my listening, I can still hear the employees, officers, and

EMTs in the skydome. There are TV station vans parked outside. Police lights find reflective surfaces to bounce around the building and into the office despite the tiniest window behind the journalist and the officer staring at us.

"What luck," the journalist says, shaking his head. "You probably would have been buried or crushed if you'd gotten out."

Hunter is nodding. I'm shaking my head.

"And your bags got switched," the officer said. "You ended up with rope."

Hunter is nodding. I'm shaking my head.

I wonder what I would do if I got home and found a surprise cupcake and ring. Would I eat it? Would I wear it? How would I find the owner? What if the young man just threw the whole thing away?

Hunter squeezes my hand and says, "Story saved me."

They are all looking at me like I am a rare artifact or a holy relic, as if they can rub my toe for luck.

"He's exaggerating," I say. "What he's not telling you is that I passed out right in the middle of it all."

Hunter rubs my finger—where there is no ring.

"Plus, I'm sure we wouldn't be in this mess if it hadn't been for me. If I hadn't had to go to Rome, or hadn't thrown the ring in the Trevi Fountain, or hadn't stormed off into a literal shit storm."

I am met with quiet disagreeing eyes.

"That's what I've been trying to say this whole time. I knew about the sinkhole, already."

TRACK 35: "I'M THE MAN WHO LOVES YOU"

Story

When I saw the cornstarch, I thought of the night Hunter came to my divorce party. I was so nervous I threw up in the bathroom. I saw the sinkhole then. I saw it. I saw the car and the hole in the ground. I saw myself tangled up in the blue devil.

When I heard the first crack, like a crack in the ice, I knew exactly what was happening. I saw the flash of me falling in. I thought, *okay, it's just me then. Hunter will be fine.* When he went to leave the car, I didn't know I grabbed him. I didn't know I was telling him to stay.

I don't remember anything after that actually, because my body betrayed me.

Hunter was experiencing the worst day of his life, and I was dreaming about my mother and father's wedding day.

I was on a showboat floating down the Ohio River. I'm pretty sure they were actually married in a church, but I wasn't alive for their wedding. I only knew it as their wedding in the dream. I was dressed like a vendor. Live music played, but it sounded like it was on a staticky radio station. The carpet was soggy. I reasoned drinks had been spilled, and I thought, *Oh no! It's my job to clean that up*. Then, as I hunted for a towel, I realized the entire floor was soaked in river water.

My mind went straight to the Titanic. The boat was sinking.

I needed to tell my parents. I spotted them on the dance floor, but I couldn't get to them. Guests were dancing in circles around them, blocking them from me.

I saw the band and yelled at the guitarist. "The boat is sinking!" She just smiled back at me.

When I looked back to the dance floor, the water was ankle high. I thought, *I have to tell them myself*. I stepped up on the stage and grabbed the microphone from the lead singer. This is mostly irrelevant, but he looked like Elvis or like an Elvis impersonator. I said, "I don't want to cause a panic, but we need to find the shore. Does anyone have any flares?" When no one turned toward me, I said, "Ladies and gentleman, it's very important we put on our life jackets." My mom and dad continued dancing, unperturbed.

Finally, I screamed, "You're all going to die!"

Everyone looked at me then. For a moment, I thought they were in shock, but then, my dad did the craziest, most dad-thing he'd ever done. He raised his glass to me. Everyone cheered like I had just toasted to the happy couple. Suddenly, there was a champagne glass in my hand. I threw it down, but it landed in the water that was waist high now. My parents were intertwining their arms as they drank their champagne, knotting themselves together.

I jumped off the stage and waded through the water. It was so cold. I mean, Titanic-cold or Ohio-river-in-February-cold.

I tried pushing through the guests, but the scene continued to morph around me. I wasn't fighting my way to the middle of a dance floor. I was fighting my way to the railing of the sinking boat. All the guests were hanging over the railing of the boat as my mom and dad got into my dad's Corvette. The car was on the surface of the water. Little tin cans bobbed on the surface until one by one they all sank. They moved from one sinking boat to the next. As my parents drove into the Ohio river, into the reflection of the sunset, everyone on the boat waved and cheered them on.

I just stood there and watched them sink. There was nothing I could do. They must have known this would happen. That they must have felt the water in the seat of the Corvette. They must have felt the cold against their skin, soaking through the fabric of the wedding gown and the tuxedo. They must have watched the water seep in through the floorboard, spilling over the gear shift and swallowing them whole. They must have let it all happen.

And then, wildly, I thought, "Their cake! They forgot their cake!"

I asked the guests around me, who were my own family and friends, "Did you get cake?"

An older man ignored my question and looped a piece of rope around me. Next, my younger cousin looped the rope across my chest. I had to bend over just so she could reach. I asked her if she had gotten some cake, and she smiled at me and nodded. One after the other, guests kissed my cheek and circled me in rope. I thought I was moving among them, but they were moving me among themselves. They were passing me on, tying me up in knots and getting me to a lifeboat. I stepped into the boat willingly. I thought these people cared about me. They were getting me off the sinking boat. They were saving me.

They pushed me out into the Ohio River, alone in my lifeboat. The guests waved goodbye to me. Lightning split the sky, and it began to rain. I watched the showboat sink and realized too late that the rope I was tied up in was tethered to the showboat. The showboat dragged me and my lifeboat under water. I took a deep breath and held it. When my smoker lungs finally gave out, I found my lungs filled with a rush of cold winter air.

There was a light filtering up from the bottom of the river. It was a great big statue of Jesus Christ. It was Butter Jesus, on fire, and I was free falling towards him.

When I landed on the bottom of the river, my feet were planted on top of a giant wedding cake. It was a multiple tier cake, shaped like a castle. I, genderless in my vendor's uniform, was tied up like a castaway, watching a savior engulfed in flames at the bottom of the Ohio River.

Hunter called to me from the bottom of the cake. I watched him slip and slide up the cake. He'd fall and laugh, and I would too, until finally he made it to the top tier next to me. I told him to untie me, to save me, and to take me away, but he just clutched my face with his cake covered hands and kissed me over and over again. Then, he blew warm air into my lungs and shook me.

I woke up to Hunter performing CPR. I was no longer in the Corvette. As I came to, I saw we were in a very, very large hole. I thought I was still dreaming until I noticed the rope hanging down from the opening of the hole and Hunter was tying it around me like a harness so that I could be hoisted out.

***

Two EMTs appear behind me. One brings peanut butter crackers and the other a ginger ale.

"Care if we check your wound?" The one with the ginger ale kneels down next to me.

I drop the blanket I am wrapped in and lift my shirt and arm so that he can look at the cut across my ribs.

"What are the odds," he says as he presses a piece of cloth soaked in something cold against me. "Right on your tattoo."

I wince.

"Slashed it right in two, didn't it?" Hunter says as he watches them.

Everyone is looking at my ribcage and nodding.

The EMT gestures for me to let down my shirt and arm. "I don't think you'll need stitches. Just keep it clean." He has a flashlight and checks my eyes. "How do you feel?"

"Fine," I say. Hunter nudges my shoulder, and I add, "a little weak."

The EMT nods and places two fingers on the pulse at my wrist. "When was the last time you ate?"

I think about it. I know I did not get the cupcake I was promised. I think back to that morning. I remember two cups of coffee but no breakfast. We must have stopped somewhere for lunch but I don't remember.

"I don't think you've eaten today," Hunter says.

Now I feel famished. It hits me like a brick wall.

"How often do you fast all day?" The EMT looks concerned, still kneeling next to me. The second EMT offers me the crackers.

"I don't," I say.

"All the time," Hunter says at the same time.

"I don't fast," I say, between bites of the peanut butter crackers. "It's not like I'm perpetually giving up food for lent."

"Would you say you get at least three meals a day?"

I shrug. "Does anybody actually get three meals a day?"

When I'm met with smirks, I elaborate. "I eat when I'm hungry. If I'm not hungry, I don't eat."

The second EMT circles around to sit on the desk and face me. She crosses her arms and asks, "Do you find that when food is in front of you, you are suddenly hungry and capable of eating quite a lot?"

I nod.

The EMT asks me, "Do you smoke?"

"I do."

The woman says, "Do you know what object permanence is?"

The words make sense to me, but I'm not sure where she is going.

"Can I suggest you prioritize putting food in front of you? I have a daughter that never thinks of food until it is in front of her. It's like it doesn't exist unless she can see it."

I want to laugh but I feel a strange familiarity.

The EMT that was kneeling rises to his feet and puts a hand on my shoulder. "Also, cigarettes can suppress your appetite. Do you remember the food pyramid when you were little? Try to eat things from it. It's not that you can't fast, but you can't live well without nutrients."

The EMT sitting on the desk adds, "Malnutrition could lead to faintness and a tendency to pass out. It can also keep your body in a heightened state of survival. Like everything is a threat."

Their radios go off. They are being requested in the skydome inside the museum. The ginger ale is left in front of me as the EMTs tell the officer that they think I am good to go home. I am mentally whiplashed by their bold claims. My father's voice tells me *cars can't run without oil.*

I eat the crackers they gave me. They are dry and crumble in my mouth like the eucharist. I barely acknowledge that the officer tells us we can go home and begs that we stay out of trouble.

"If you're going to propose again, call me," the journalist hands Hunter a business card.

TRACK 36: "RADIO, RADIO"

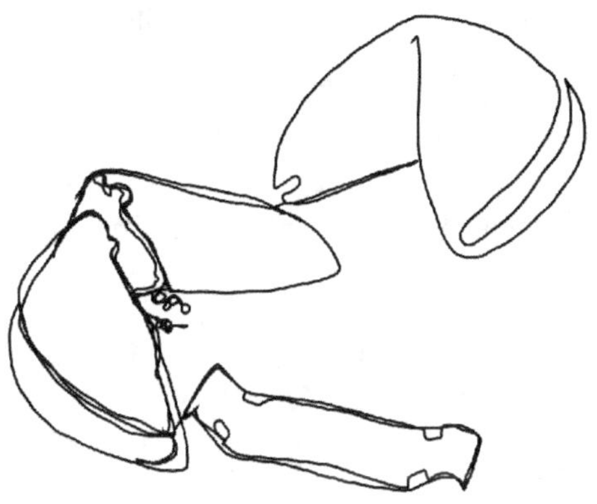

We have just filled our plates at an all-you-can-eat Chinese buffet. It has been days since the last time Hunter almost proposed to me. He is singing along with whatever is playing over the speakers of the restaurant. When he sings, he skips ahead. He always sings the next line of the song just a few moments before he should, like he is predicting it.

"Question," he asks as we sit down at a table in the middle of the mostly empty restaurant.

"Shoot," I say.

"Which do you think comes first: the movie or the soundtrack?"

"I don't understand."

"Like, the chicken or the egg. Do you think that a story comes from music or that music comes from a story? Like, *Reservoir Dogs* when

'Stuck in the Middle with You' plays. Do you think Tarantino was imagining a man cutting another man's ear off and one day, he finally found the rest of the movie?"

I drink from my cup, washing the Chinese food down. "You're thinking about Mr. Blonde's torture soundtrack right now?"

Hunter apologizes and elaborates. "What if one thing manifests into the other. You hear a song, and then you envision a thing happening. Over time the rest of the story falls into place."

I flinch at the words *story falls into place.* I waver between the ever-present possibility of being swallowed by the earth and knowing that I already survived it once. There have been flight attendants who survived a plane crash, only to continue flying and survive a second plane crash.

"Did I ever play my show for you from my guest spot in San Francisco? Right before we met?" Hunter's questions are hitting me all at once. I'm finding it hard to focus, so I eat. Visions of the rest area outside San Francisco come to me—in his van and with his phone. My gaze falls on his hands, cutting his sweet and spicy chicken at the table across from me. The words *damn right, they'll rise again* pulse in the florescent light of the restaurant.

I shake my head, no. "I don't think I heard your playlist."

He smiles at me and says, "I think the soundtrack inspires the movie." His fork clatters against the table as he abandons it and leans towards me over his plate. "I think I saw this very moment." He looks around at the oriental decor, the paper flags and lanterns, and the California roll still steaming on my plate. "It came to me when this song played."

I listen very closely.

"Not this song," he corrects. "Another song."

"What happened during the song?"

"I reunited with you." He's smiling like a mad man.

"Me?"

"Well, I didn't know it was you, but yes, you."

"What, like, déjà vu?"

He shakes his head no. "Remember the quote by Bob Dylan: *No man has ever done anything that a woman hasn't allowed or encouraged him to do.* I've always thought of Eve. I've always thought about how she ate the fruit and got Adam to eat the fruit."

"And how she originated sin," I add, "lost all future generations the pleasures of paradise, gave us painful birth and hard labor, and generally made a mess of things for the rest of the human race?"

He laughs. "Sure, that's one way to look at it. I know there is a significant portion of the population that agrees with you, but I've always been jealous of her. I think maybe she knew if it wasn't her who ate the fruit, it would be the next generation or the generation after that. She knew it was there for a reason. Someone had to eventually succumb. Someone would experience that first bite of sin. You know what I think she did? I think she said to herself, 'I want it to be me.' "

I choke on a dumpling, and he offers me a napkin. "Let me get this straight." I set my napkin and fork down to focus all my energy on what he is saying. "Are we calling her a martyr or a rebel?"

"Both," Hunter says.

"And Adam has Stockholm syndrome?" I ask.

He laughs and thinks for a moment. "Adam and Eve used to be the same person. Eve came from Adam. Gender here is just the inconvenience of grammar. It's not delineating anything. They come from the same thing."

I say, "Technically, we all come from a sperm and an egg."

"Yes!" Hunter slaps his hands on the table. "An original is broken in half and reunited in the uterus. The two halves work together, eat the apple together, and procreate together. An everlasting loop of halves looking for the whole."

"I can't tell if you're saying we are soul mates or second cousins."

The house speakers in the restaurant are playing a top country hit. Both of our plates are filled with cold food, and our waiter drops off a check without asking if we need refills.

Hunter offers me my fortune cookie. I am hesitant to know anything about my future. What if life is just an everlasting loop of broken pieces? I crack it open and smudge the black ink with a greasy thumb. It reads: *You are a lover of words. You will write a book.*

I want to tell Hunter about it, but he is smiling at his own fortune.

"What?" I ask.

He adjusts himself in his seat and pushes our plates aside. He doesn't stand up. His hands hunt for mine. He asks me point blank, "Will you marry me?"

I wonder what in the hell his fortune cookie told him. I hold back a smile and narrow my eyes at him. "No ring?"

His face falters and then bounces back. "Rings are overrated."

"Do you expect me to wear a white wedding dress?"

"Absolutely not."

"Good," I say. " 'Cause I want to wear blue."

"Of course," he says. "Your something-blue, I presume."

"For good luck," I say in affirmation.

"Naturally." He smiles, still holding my hands.

"Your mother won't approve."

"Probably not," he says, smiling.

"You want to marry me?" I ask.

"Who's proposing to who?"

I snort.

"Yes," he says. "If you're looking for an answer."

"You're telling me how to answer you?"

"No, I'm answering your question." He coughs. "Since you're not answering mine."

"You want to tie the knot?"

His grip loosens as he laughs, but he doesn't let go. "Yes."

"You want the proverbial ball and chain?"

"Yes."

"You want to swear your undying love for me in front of our family and friends?"

"Yes."

"You want to give up this Garden of Eden?" I look around the air-conditioned dining room. There is a small family of five in the far corner with an infant in a high chair who is looking at a man who eats alone with his trucker hat on the table next to his food. "You want me to eat the fruit of the tree of good and evil?"

"Yes … wait." He stops. "Am I Eve or Adam in this scenario?"

I shrug.

"Yes," he says, as if it applies either way.

My lips restrain my smile like a straitjacket, like joy is dangerous when unconfined.

He rubs his fingers along my knuckles. "You're killin' me here."

His wrist is still wrapped in an ace bandage. He has a pink mark over his left temple where he picked a scab too early. His hair is clean but disheveled because we have slept at home for days, resting. I have been killing him and he has been killing me, all this time. And yet, he has brought me here, so that together we may eat our hearts out, fill our bellies, and not pass out from malnutrition.

He smiles and leans forward to kiss my hand. A song comes on the radio over the speakers in the Chinese restaurant. His face illuminates with surprise. "This one! This is the song that inspired visions of you!"

I hear the dirty guitar of "She Don't Use Jelly" by the Flaming Lips. As the song plays and I listen to the lyrics, I can see myself in my old apartment bathroom on the eve of a new year. My feverish reflection is in the mirror, and I know it is Hunter just beyond the door.

"Okay," I say. "Let's blow up some cake."

EPILOGUE

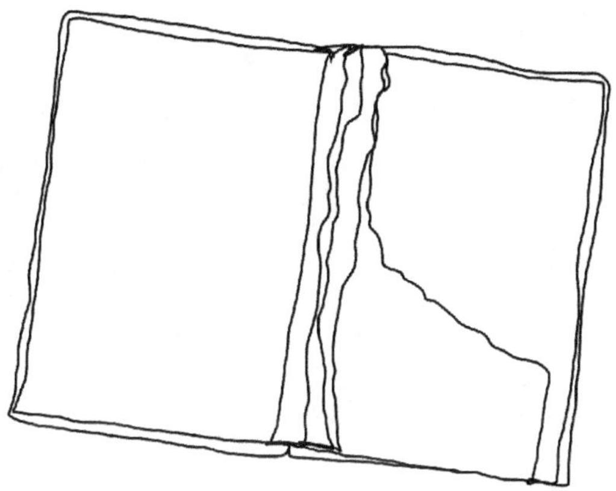

A song once told me to rip the epilogues out of the books that I had read. So I did.

NOTES TO THE READER

The chapters in this book are real song titles. A playlist can be found on my website, Spotify, and Apple Music by both myself and fans.

I have written an epilogue for Story & Hunter. You can read it by subscribing (for free) to my website. Subscribing tells me two things: first, you loved (or sort of liked?) the book and want more from the characters (or me) and second, you don't mind receiving the occasional (rare) email to let you know about book events, sales, and upcoming projects.

If I can also ask you, dear reader, for one favor: please review *They Won't Apologize for the Mess* on Goodreads or the platform of your choice.

ACKNOWLEDGEMENTS

I owe a lot to C.D. Hunt. This book and my love for writing would not be, had she not encouraged me to participate in NaNoWriMo in 2019. A thank you must also go to Lexington Ladies Lit for taking a chance on my ARC in 2022 and memorializing it on their tote bag. Thank you to Amanda for many things, but specifically for bringing the ladies of book club into my life. Thank you, Stephanie, for editing my first mess.

I also want to thank Lisa for beta-reading and giving me tons of notes, C.D. Hunt, again, for reading so many versions of this story. Cory for suffering through a poorly disguised Keith Stanton, Amy and Alison for their notes and encouragement, Alison, again, for entertaining my slightly unhinged aspirations and copyediting, and Hilary for calling my book "sexy." You've always made me feel seen.

I am thankful for so many friends who offered to read, did read, and reviewed the unedited version of this novel. Thank you to everyone in my life who has encouraged me to dig this story up and to give it a spot in the light.

Thank you, Mom, for literally everything. Thank you, Josh, for being a constant inspiration and steady companion.

ABOUT THE AUTHOR

Xine grew up in the foothills of Eastern Kentucky, on the threshold of Appalachia, neither coming or going. She writes poetry, prose, and screenplays. She studied at Eastern Kentucky University, Savannah College of Art and Design, Oxford, and UCLAx. When she is not writing, she hopes to be found in airports or on the sets of music videos and short films. This is her debut novel. Her other written work can be found in various publications.